CW00547827

CC

# Days of Death

Elwood Black wants complete control over the gold mining community of Thomaston. He surrounds himself with killers such as Clive Carter, outlaw and deadly gunman, and the Goliath-like pugilist, Sheriff Goran Ginsberg. He makes one fatal mistake – his man Carter kills Cyriac Halkias' brother. Heavily scarred from previous deadly encounters, Cyriac rides to Thomaston. Those responsible for his brother's death must pay. The body count mounts as the days of death descend on Thomaston. Cyriac will not stop until the account of his vengeance has been paid in full.

# Days of Death

P. McCormac

A Black Horse Western

ROBERT HALE

ISBN 978-0-7198-2099-1

The Crowood Press
The Stable Block
Crowood Lane
Ramsbury
Marlborough
Wiltshire SN8 2HR

www.bhwesterns.com

Robert Hale is an imprint
of The Crowood Press

Typeset by
Derek Doyle & Associates, Shaw Heath
Printed and bound in Great Britain by
CPI Group (UK) Ltd, Croydon, CR0 4YY

# 1

Turlough lay on his stomach and screwing his features into a grimace of pain, gingerly dabbed at the scalp wound with a wad of moss torn from the boulders on the side of the pool. Again and again he dipped the moss into the water and gently swabbed the lacerations, wincing each time the pad touched the tender punctures. Then he sluiced his face in the clear cold water. As he did so he became aware of a movement almost directly opposite. His body froze and a moment of fear lurched in his chest. If it was them, he knew he was as good as dead.

Slowly, fearfully, his eyes travelled up the sapling-covered slope. Squatting opposite, quietly watching him was a stranger. About thirty yards separated them. Silently they stared at each other across the intervening distance. Turlough's fear grew within as he noted the rifle held loosely in the man's hands. Cautiously he raised himself and sat back on his heels.

Turlough was a burly youth with square manly features and a steady manner which gave him an air of gentle reserve. He was slow to anger and patient in even the most taxing circumstances. Now he squinted anxiously up the slope at the man in the trees. He couldn't quite make out the face of the stranger, but had an impression of long narrow features covered with a straggly beard.

'You in some kind of trouble, son?'

Turlough stared back in silence for a moment before replying.

'I fell and hurt my head. Can't seem to remember who I am,' he lied. 'Where's this place?'

'Cullbeg Pass,' came the reply.

Cullbeg Pass. Had he come far enough to escape them? Probably not. They would come after him. They would hunt him until the death. Turlough stared into the surrounding trees acting vague and lost. The bearded man stood up, the rifle hanging slackly from one hand.

'Come,' he gestured with his free hand. 'You look as if you need a mite of help.'

Obediently Turlough stood and waded across the narrow stream. As he came closer to the stranger he noted the slight build of the man. The stranger pointed up the slope. Turlough nodded and stepped forward to pass him. As he did so he lunged sideways and grabbed for the rifle. Turlough felt rather than saw the hard knee that hit him in the chest and then he was sprawling on the ground, trying desperately to catch his breath and scrabbling at the earth to prevent himself from rolling back down the slope and into the stream.

'What in tarnation's the matter with you, boy? I'm offering to help you and you attack me. Is there no gratitude in people these days?'

Turlough had come to rest against the base of a young tree and lay there gasping and looking fearfully at the bearded stranger. He expected the man to use the rifle either to hit him or shoot him. But the man only stood there looking down at him for a moment before turning and walking back up the slope.

'Wait! Wait!' gasped Turlough, struggling to rise. 'I'm

sorry, I do need help.'

He went crawling after the stranger, desperately clawing his way up the slope. But the man was gone. Like a wraith of the woods he had vanished. Turlough reached the crest of the slope, panting heavily. Anxiously, he probed the woods for sight of the stranger. All was silent and still around him. It was as if he was the only person left in the world.

Wearily Turlough sank back and cursed his own clumsiness. The wound in his head had slowed him down more than he knew. He should have been able to wrest the rifle from the man and force him to assist him. Now his inept attempt had only made him worse off. All he had done was make another enemy. There were enemies aplenty at this moment somewhere out there hunting him.

He surveyed the woods again. Should he track the man down and wait for a moment to catch him off guard? He must live nearby. Perhaps he had been out hunting; that would account for the rifle. But what direction had he gone? Turlough cast around him but could find no obvious trail. He set out once more through the woods.

The wound in his head throbbed steadily, making him feel sick and exhausted. The woods were silent and he was painfully aware of his own clumsy passage through the trees. He tried to ease his footfalls but that only slowed him down. Leaves and twigs crunched beneath his feet and branches jarred painfully against his body as he passed. On and on he stumbled – one weary step after another. When he saw the rabbit hanging in the snare he stopped, hardly believing his luck. Eagerly he stepped forward, then slowed and nervously examined the surrounding foliage – nothing moved – nothing stirred. He was alone and ravenous in the woods, with a dead rabbit hanging in a snare. There was only one course of action.

7

He went forward cautiously and kneeling beside the noose, began to untangle the small mammal. When the cold, round thing pressed against his neck he knew instinctively what it was and who was behind him.

'Jeez,' he whimpered. 'Don't kill me.'

'It's not Jesus, my ungrateful friend. Not only do you attack someone who is about to help you but you steal from traps as well. On top of that you are a blasphemer, taking the name of the Lord in vain. What other crimes are you capable of?'

'I didn't mean any harm.'

He felt something touch his hair and he jerked away.

'Hold still while I examine that injury,' an impatient voice ordered.

He crouched, trembling as gentle fingers explored his head wound.

'If I'm any judge of injuries that's a shotgun wound.'

Turlough winced as the fingers probed delicately.

'I thought so; some of the pellets are still in the scalp.'

The pressure of the gun on his neck eased and he knew the man had stepped away.

'What poor critter had to protect themselves from you with a shotgun?'

Slowly Turlough turned and saw the bearded man leaning casually against a tree with the rifle slung carelessly beneath one arm. Briefly Turlough wondered if he would be quick enough to tackle the man before he could bring the gun up.

'The barrel of this rifle will crack open the other side of that thick skull if you try another dumb-ass attack.'

Turlough blinked foolishly and then sank to the ground. This man seemed able to anticipate his every move. He shrugged hopelessly and sighed. All the fight suddenly went from him.

8

'I'm sorry,' he mumbled, 'I was shot and I'm on the run from them as did it. When they catch me they'll finish the job. I thought if I could get hold of your gun I would stand a better chance against them.'

'What is it – angry father found you with his daughter or what?'

'No, nothing like that. Just a private matter.' Turlough looked up at the stranger. 'All I need is some food and a rest and then I'll go on and not bother you again.'

'Who's after you?'

Turlough hung his head. 'I can't tell you.'

'Pick up that rabbit and head over in that direction.'

The man pointed and Turlough did as he was told. They progressed steadily until at one point the man told him to stop.

'I'll have to blindfold you. It's just so you won't be able to track me.'

Turlough stood docile while he was blindfolded. He felt the gun barrel being pushed into his hand.

'Hold on to that. If you jerk or pull it'll go off.'

Thus they proceeded – Turlough blindfolded, stumbling in the wake of the stranger, and holding on to a rifle barrel.

Turlough lay where he was for a time, nursing the ache in his head. After a while he hoisted himself on to his elbows. At once he wished he hadn't. Pain lanced across the top of his skull and he moaned aloud.

'Ah, Jeez! I wish I was dead.'

Then he remembered his flight from the mine workings and immediately regretted the sentiment. When his surroundings stopped spinning and the ache in his head eased slightly he looked around. His host was nowhere to be seen.

Last night he had led Turlough blindfolded through the woods. When they stopped the man had given him a slug from his canteen. Instead of water it contained raw moonshine. The brew had seared a fiery track from his throat to his abdomen before radiating a warm glow within him. After that he must have passed out, oblivious of everything until this morning.

The youngster remembered the stranger had been working on the wound in his head when he had passed out. Gently he felt around his scalp and realized the injury now had a dressing.

'Does that booger think he's some sort of doctor?'

Turlough surveyed his surroundings. There was nothing to indicate a dwelling or camp of any description. He concluded that his morose companion lived elsewhere and had brought him here for safety or for seclusion. The man had supplied a bed of soft grasses and a dirty blanket that covered the youngster from the elements.

Slowly, so as not to jar his aching head, he rolled over and got cautiously to his feet. He had a great need of a drink and an urge to follow the call of nature. Tiredly he walked into the surrounding underbrush and trees.

Finding a concealed place, Turlough lowered his trousers and squatted down, his eyes darting around as he did so. He relaxed somewhat as he settled and thought about the bearded man.

Turlough wondered if he was a deserter from the army. The competent way he handled himself all pointed to this conclusion. The man had made a sanctuary for himself and was living off the land. If he was a deserter he would be lying low and that would suit Turlough admirably.

Perhaps the stranger would let him stay. He certainly wasn't unfriendly. In spite of his gruff manner he had taken care of Turlough and also gave him shelter of a kind.

In the midst of his musings the gunshots startled him. Turlough leapt to his feet. The sudden movement started the waves of pain in his head again. Cursing under his breath he struggled into his pants and then crouched low, peering in the direction of the shots. There were shouts and then more gunfire.

Someone came crashing into the clearing and Turlough saw it was his mystery rescuer. Suddenly there were figures swarming all over the clearing. Men in duster coats wearing black Stetsons and all pointing rifles at the man they had cornered. Turlough's heart, already beating fast, now sped up by several degrees. His nemesis had arrived. This was the nightmare that had pursued him into these woods.

The stranger, realizing he was surrounded, stopped moving and watched cautiously as the men circled around him. Turlough saw the blood dripping on the grass from the man's left hand.

He reminded Turlough of an animal at bay, trapped by the hunters. Turlough could see his eyes flicking from side to side, weighing up his chances. But it was hopeless. The ring of menacing figures closed tight around the man.

Turlough chewed his lip and frowned down at the men who were pursuing him. He watched as a rifle butt hit the cornered man from behind. The man staggered and sagged to his knees.

With a swift movement, the leader stepped forward and swiped the butt of his rifle against the side of the fugitive's head. Turlough saw the wounded man try to roll with the

11

blow but he went down heavily.

'Bastard!' grunted the man who had struck out.

Turlough knew them, knew it was him they were after.

'Where is he?'

The hurt man mumbled something Turlough couldn't make out. Viciously the interrogator kicked the man in the groin. Turlough winced as he saw his rescuer curl up with a low groan.

'Don't mess with me! You must have seen him. We tracked him this way.'

Another kick emphasized the questions. The gunman raised his weapon.

'First I'll shoot you in the shoulder, then in the knees. I'll carry on like that till you tell me where he is.'

The shot rang out and the man on the ground jerked and cried out as the slug hit him.

Turlough knew these men were capable of carrying out their threats. Chewing vigorously at his lower lip, he peered through the leaves at the scene in the clearing. The man on the ground was trying to raise himself up. He was kicked in the side for his efforts. Turlough knew they were going to kill the man, no matter what he told them.

It would make no difference whether or not they got the information out of him. That was how they worked. Threats, intimidation, killing, all came second nature to them. That was how they survived. They lived on the fear of others, committing dreadful and foul deeds so that the dread of inviting their attention acted like a mantle of compliance so that no one crossed them.

Turlough knew, looking now at their dark threatening forms, they were after him and they would keep tracking him until they found him. They would not kill him immediately. They would take him back, subject him to brutal torture and hang his body up as a warning to others.

Turlough's fingers searched the dirt, looking for a missile of some sort. Carefully he loosened a moss-covered rock about the size of his fist. Slowly he rose to his feet. He knew he should creep away and try to outrun his pursuers again. But the man down there had helped him and Turlough's sense of fair play indicated that he owed him.

With an eye that had hurled stones at birds and small animals with unerring accuracy, he measured distances and velocity. Slowly he drew back his arm. The stone curved through the air, turning over and over and plunged into the clearing.

It took the leader of the gunmen in the ear and hit him sideways. As he fell, his trigger finger tightened, and a bullet from the weapon tore into the thigh of the gunman holding their prisoner.

Once he saw the result of his missile, Turlough turned and plunged through the woods. He had done what he had to do and now his own skin was in danger once more. On he fled and in his great fear he forgot his wounded head and his injuries and thought only of flight.

Crashing through the woods, he never thought once to look behind, for he knew there would be no point. It would be a certainty the armed men would be pursuing him.

Bushes reached out and snagged his legs as he stumbled along a non-existent pathway. In his headlong flight, he crashed into trees – tripped up and fell, his body labouring as he forced himself to get up and go on. What a fool he had been to intervene. He could not even be sure if his action would have saved the man who had helped him.

He had seen the rock strike the leader and the effects of his reflex action on his trigger finger. Beyond that he knew only that in the next half hour or even less he would be caught and dragged back to agonizing torture and a gruesome end.

He ran on only because he would not give up easily. While he could still run he would flee like a wounded animal till they cornered him. Only then would he turn and fight till they clubbed him into unconsciousness. With luck they would kill him out here in the woods. It was the only way he would hope to avoid the barbarities that lay in store for him.

Turlough's legs were beginning to falter. His breathing hurt his chest and his head was a jagged fireball of pain. Still he laboured on, forcing one leg in front of the other. He thought not of concealment, only of flight – the flight of a wounded animal running in terror from the hunt.

The hunted animal didn't know the fate that lay ahead; couldn't anticipate the death that would bring oblivion. The hunted animal would run, using cunning and wiles to avoid capture. When it was caught it would accept its fate and die. Turlough had no such processes of insensitivity. He knew only too well what he faced. And then there was no ground underneath his flailing feet.

As he fell, Turlough tried to get his feet under him but it was a futile effort. He tumbled over and then crashed face first to earth. For a few moments he lay winded and unmoving. Branches, grass and dirt rained down upon him from where he had hit the edge of the overhang. He was too breathless to do anything but lie there, waiting for the breath to come back into his bruised and battered body.

While he did this he felt the ground move beneath him. It was the slow menacing heave of a prehistoric organism. At the same time he heard the shouts above and around him.

'Can you see the bastard?'

'No sign of him!'

'Keep looking, he can't have gone far.'

'Don't kill him. We want him alive.'

'Do you hear me, Benedict? You're dead meat! But before that we'll make you suffer.'

Turlough heard the shouted threats. He lay perfectly still, unaware that no one could see him. The branches and leaves that had showered down when he fell camouflaged him, breaking up the outline of his body. By keeping still he blended perfectly with his surroundings. The reason he was afraid to move was the terror engendered by the slow gargantuan movements beneath his bruised and winded body.

'Plug!'

Beside him in the mud, a small orifice puckered and a puff of marsh gas vented into the air. Escape or not, Turlough could not move. His body was locked in the paralysis of fright. He lay motionless and felt the slime of the swamp seeping into his clothing and creeping across his body. Slowly he opened his eyes, which up till then he had been keeping tightly shut. Around him the peace of the woodland was gradually restored as the marauding gunmen searched further afield for their quarry.

'Plug!'

Another whiff of gas escaped. A mental picture of the bog opening its swampy mouth and sucking him into its black interior was conjured up in his mind.

Turlough chewed over his fate. If he stayed where he

15

was, spread-eagled on the swamp, he would slowly sink into the black mass of mud. It would be an unhurried suffocation. Mud creeping into his eyes, mouth, ears and nose. He contemplated the final gasping struggles as he tried to keep his mouth and nose free from the invasive mud.

He sighed – a huge shuddering sigh. Perhaps it was all for the best. It would certainly be a less frightening death than awaited him if captured by the men hunting him.

The woods were quiet now. Turlough raised his head slightly. He was terrified to move any other part of his body. His eyes flicked around as he contemplated his surroundings. Not far from his outstretched arms, he spied something that raised a faint flicker of hope. A long tapering root had forced its way out of the overhang from which he had fallen. In its search for nourishment, the root had stretched down into the swamp. This root, thin and fibrous, offered a glimmer of hope.

Could it be . . . would it just be possible to grasp that rootlet and use it to pull himself free of his glutinous plight? He began the tentative movement of one hand towards that slender tendril of uncertain salvation.

A nerve-wracking half hour later, Turlough pulled himself hand over hand up that fibrous root. Near the top of the overhang, his fingers scrabbled for a grip and found long coarse grass that gave him some purchase. Only the great strength in his arms and hands finally took him over the rim.

For long agonizing moments, he lay at rest with his legs hanging out over the edge. Then gradually he wriggled the last few feet to safety. He rolled over on his back and just lay there, his chest heaving and sweat and mud drying on his body.

In time, Turlough was able to roll back on to his front and clamber to his feet. If he was to survive he had to find the man's cabin and kit himself out with supplies. He regretted the stranger's death, for he was certain the raiders would have killed him. For long moments he stayed where he was, listening, but there was nothing to indicate the hunters had returned. Birds called from high up in the trees and an animal coughed somewhere over to his right. In the place of the raucous incursion of the human hunters, the sounds of nature were gradually reasserting itself.

Cautiously, Turlough retraced his steps to the place he had last beheld the stranger being beaten. The body was still lying where it had fallen and he slid down the side of dip where it was located. There was nothing he could do for the poor soul but odious as it was, Turlough needed to search the body for some clue as to where the man had been living, though that seemed unlikely. Maybe there might be something useful to be found, like a knife or tobacco. He cast around without much hope for the man's rifle but without result. At last he knelt by the motionless form lying face down.

The youngster tugged at the jacket, pulling it from underneath the body. In one pocket he found cartridges and a few pieces of leather. In an inside pocket he found a well used Bible and strips of rawhide. At last he found the makings and sat by the body and built himself a smoke. While he smoked, he idly opened the Bible. Inside the name Milo Halkias was printed. Beneath the name were the words *D.O.B. 27 May 1851.*

'Well, Milo Halkias, if this is your writing that makes you thirty-three. Seems a mite young to die. Another seventeen years and you could have seen in the new century. I guess I brought this on you, seeing as the men as killed you were seeking me and found you instead. The least I can do is give you a decent burial.'

17

Turlough thought of the swamp he had just escaped from and wondered if it was disrespectful to bury the dead man in that. It would certainly save a lot of digging considering he had no tools at hand.

'What am I to do with you, Milo? I'd like to think I would do the right thing by you. Firstly I rob you of your life by bringing Clive Carter and his band of killers here and now I'm stealing your possessions. You must think me an ornery piece of lowlife.'

Turlough sighed deeply. Finishing his smoke, he gripped the body and flipped it over. He saw the handle of a Bowie knife and plucked that from a sheath attached to a leather belt. On reflection he undid the belt and tugged that free. As he did so he noticed something poking out from under the shirt. Curious, he undid the shirt and was surprised to find a money belt.

'I wonder what you keep in this,' he grunted as he undid the belt and tugged it free. Moments later he sat back on his heels and whistled.

'I'll carry a mule to Kentucky!' he exclaimed.

The pockets were stuffed with banknotes. And while he wondered about his good fortune, the dead body he had been robbing groaned.

Turlough sank back on his heels and stared at the face of the man lying so pale and still.

'By the dead, but you're still alive.'

How easy would it be to snuff out that flickering candle, he thought. He could walk from here a rich man and buy himself a new existence far away from the death that even now was somewhere out there stalking him. With the money in the belt he could even hire bodyguards to protect him from his enemies. But something stayed his hand – like conscience or some misguided sentiment. With a sigh, he set to work to move Milo to a more sheltered place.

After some effort of sweat and hurt he managed to drag his charge to the very place he himself had lain last night. When he had made Milo as comfortable as possible, Turlough retraced his steps to the stream where he had originally encountered Milo. He submerged his face and drank before filling the man's hat with water and trudging back again.

The youngster bathed Milo's face and then trickled water into his mouth. As the water went in his patient gulped a time or two and swallowed convulsively but did not awaken.

'Well, fella, by rights you should be dead but somehow you ain't. By rights I should be dead but I ain't.' Turlough chortled mirthlessly. 'We may be not in great shape but at least we are rich, or at least you are. Much good that will do us out here. What we need is a few medical supplies and several bottles of bourbon but I can't see no store hereabouts.

'I need to find your hidey-hole. I guess you have food and stuff hoarded up there that would make life a mite easier for us both. I'll have a scout around and see if I can locate it.' Turlough stood, feeling his aches as he did so. 'Just you lie there quiet like and I'll be back when I can.'

After going round in circles without finding any sign of a dwelling, Turlough gave up and returning to his patient, squatted down beside him.

'Guess we'll just have to go without. I'm no tracker or I should have found your den by now. Your chances of survival are considerably lessened the more you have to lie out here.'

Turlough's stomach rumbled and he massaged it, trying to tone down the hunger pains.

'Sure could do with some decent food and drink. I guess we'll both perish sitting out here on this damn hill.'

He glanced down at Milo and was surprised to find a pair of cold blue eyes regarding him.

'You awake, fella?'

He got a groan in reply and Milo tried to lift his head but groaned again and dropped back.

'I can take you to your shack, wherever that is. Just give me directions and I'll do my best to get you there.'

He caught a whisper of sound and bent close.

'How can I trust someone as steals my money belt?'

Turlough glanced guiltily at the money belt. He had been fiddling with it as he contemplated his chances of survival.

'I . . . I thought you were dead. I was just keeping it safe for you. Look, you're hurt bad. I need to get you to shelter. Get you warm and get some food in you.'

There was no reply and Turlough anxiously studied the injured man's face.

'I don't think I can make it,' the whisper came again. 'Are you strong enough to carry me?'

'I guess so. I been knocked about a bit but if it ain't far I'll do my best.'

With Milo slung across his back, Turlough got to the hideout which turned out to be a cave screened by a dense growth of bush and tree. He staggered inside and collapsed, rolling over to dislodge his burden. It was several minutes before he recovered enough to examine the refuge.

In the faint light that filtered in he found a lamp which

he lit and looked around him. By the entrance was a blackened circle of stones and a store of dry wood so he got a fire going. There was very little smoke but he was nervous all the same, thinking of the men hunting him.

Turlough propped Milo up and tried to get him to drink some hot coffee but most of it dribbled down on his shirt. The colour had gone from his face and his breathing was hardly discernible. He wrapped him in blankets, thinking the warmth might help him. For himself he heated beans and chewed jerky, dousing the fire when he had finished cooking. It was only then that he explored the cave.

He was immediately rewarded by finding a Smith & Wesson revolver in a holster. When he found Milo confronted by Carver and his men, there had been no sign of the rifle he had been carrying. Turlough could only speculate that his attackers had taken it. He searched for, and found shells for the handgun and the rifle. Pushing the gun inside his waistband, he continued searching. There was food enough to last some days if he eked it out. Then he discovered an almost full bottle of whiskey labelled Coffin Varnish.

'I guess that about suits this predicament I find myself in,' Turlough muttered as he pulled the cork and took a swig.

If he had taken a mouthful of kerosene it might have tasted better, but Turlough managed to swallow it down, feeling it burn a track all the way into his belly.

'Wow!' he gasped, his eyes watering as he bent over trying to catch his breath. 'I reckon a fella has to get used to this kinda rotgut.'

He gazed speculatively at the man covered over with blankets and then back at the whiskey bottle in his hand.

'I wonder if. . . .' Turlough hunkered down by his companion and eased his head up. 'There now, buddy, this is kill or cure time.'

He offered up the bottle to Milo, pressing it between his lips and gently tipping so some ran into his slack mouth. It was much the same result as with the coffee. Some went in his mouth but most dribbled down his chin and on to his shirt. Turlough sensed a movement behind him and turned quickly.

A huge shape loomed up and he saw something swing towards him. He tried to duck but there was not time. He felt a tremendous blow on the side of his head and was falling. Even as he hit the rough floor, he was clawing at the Smith & Wesson in his belt. The gun was kicked from his hand and he was picked up and thrown against the wall of the cave.

His senses swimming, he crawled towards the entrance but something crunched into the back of his head and he went down. His face hit the rocky floor and there was an intense flare of numbing pain before he passed out.

His head was a throbbing cauldron of agony – his mouth was stuffed with cotton wool and a saw was ripping slices off the top of his skull. Turlough whimpered as waves of nausea swept through him. Slowly he opened his eyes and recollection returned as he made out the interior of the cave.

Something had attacked him as he ministered to the wounded stranger. From his fleeting glimpse of the bulky shape, he suspected it was a bear. He kept perfectly still but it was to no avail. The creature must have heard his moan as he came to, and there was movement within the cave and the thing loomed over him. Turlough closed his eyes again and feigned death which was easy enough as that was how he was feeling – more dead than alive.

It was to no avail. Something gripped him by his shirt front and hauled him upright. Turlough kept his eyes tightly closed. That did not work, either. Something that felt like a hunk of beef hit him across the face.

'Damn it,' he groaned and opened his eyes to see the ugliest countenance it had ever been his bad luck to encounter.

'You're gonna pay for this,' a voice like a coffee bean grinder in action told him.

Again that wedge of beef hit him, only this time his eyes were open and he could see it was not beef but the meaty hand of the man holding him upright. The world went out of focus and his head wobbled about on his neck while the contents of his skull broke loose and rattled about, causing excruciating agony. As if to even up the beating he was hit on the other cheek, loosening some teeth as well as causing him to drift towards unconsciousness once more. There was more of that grinding interrogation, mostly unintelligible.

Turlough felt himself being dragged across the cave floor and propped against the wall. As he tried to gather his wits – an almost impossible task with the agonizing throbbing in his head, he reluctantly opened his eyes to see the brute squatting in front of him.

'Don't hit me again,' he pleaded, slurring his words because his mouth was hurting so much along with everything else in his body.

'Start talking. How did you find us? Did someone blab on us?'

'No, no it wasn't like that. That man – your friend, Milo, was helping me when we were attacked. I was trying to take care of him.'

The large head turned slightly as the brute glanced over his shoulder.

'Why'd you steal the money?'

'Look, you got this all wrong. Some people were chasing me. Milo rescued me but they beat him pretty bad. I dragged him in here to try and save him.'

Turlough's head banged against the wall as he was hit again. This time it took longer for his eyes to focus.

'You're lying. You beat him to make him tell about the hideout and the money. Once you got him in here you needed to find out who else was in on it, but he passed out afore you got all the information. You were feeding him whiskey to revive him so as you get the dope on his accomplices. Who are you? Are you a bounty hunter?'

'Hell, no! It's as I told you. I was pretty far gone when Milo found me and patched me up,' Turlough babbled. 'Then these other fellas came and roughed him up. They wanted to find out about me. It was only as I was trying to revive him I found the money. I weren't stealing it, I was taking care of it for him. One good turn deserves another. I could have left him out there to die but I didn't do that. He told me how to find this place so I carried him in here. That's the truth so help me God.'

Turlough was talking as fast as his stiff and aching jaws would allow, fearful of another bone-jarring slap from his interrogator. Eyes like black opals gazed steadfastly at him and Turlough felt they could see into his very soul. This close up he could see a face much disfigured by old wounds. As if the face had been smashed up and patched together again.

One scar ran at an angle from the hairline across the

top of the nose and into the opposite cheek. One eye
seemed at a different level from its mate. The nose had
been broken in two places and jutted angularly in different
directions. Another scar ran from the left ear and disappeared into the corner of the mouth. It was a face from a
nightmare and it was inches from Turlough's own. In spite
of himself he shuddered.

Helplessly Turlough stared into those gimlet eyes and
saw death lurking there. That big scarred hand reached
out and closed around Turlough's throat. It was like being
gripped by a cast iron manacle. Turlough kept very still. He
knew this man could squeeze the life from him as easily as
he would squash a bug.

'Give me one reason why I should believe you. Or give
me one good reason why I should not kill you.'

'I . . . I could help you take care of Milo – until he recov-
ers that is. He'll tell you I'm speaking the truth.'

Turlough knew his voice was quaking with fright but
could not help it. Even the men pursuing him did not
engender as much terror as this indomitable creature squatting before him – seemingly ready to snuff out his life as
easily as he would extinguish the flame of a guttering candle.

The clamp on his throat tightened and Turlough
stopped breathing. As he felt that bone hard grip on his
windpipe he thought of all the things he wanted to do but
would never do now.

He had dreamed of going East and walking through the
streets of a big city. What would it be like to stand on the
eastern seaboard and look out over the vast expanse of the
Atlantic Ocean? He had never felt the softness of a
woman's touch on his body. And then he wondered if
anyone would miss him. He had left his family back in Gold
Point. Now he would never see them again.

The vice tightened and Turlough's regrets ended and

he struggled helplessly against that iron clutch that bit by bit was choking off his breathing.

**6**

The choke grip loosened and Turlough sagged against the cave wall, sucking in life-giving air. He watched apprehensively as his nemesis turned without a word and moved away. If he thought he was being spared he was mistaken. The big man returned with a coil of rawhide. Roughly he gripped Turlough's hands and deftly bound his wrists together and then did the same to his ankles.

'What are you gonna do with me?" Turlough asked.

He might as well not have wasted his precious breath. Without answering the man went across to where his injured companion lay and after examining him, turned and left the cave.

Turlough tested his bonds but they were very secure. Indeed, so tightly bound was he that the circulation to his hands and feet was severely restricted. Amongst all the other throbbing hurts in his body this was but another discomfort to endure. He resigned himself to the fact he was completely at the mercy of the taciturn stranger.

He must have dozed off as he awoke to find his captor untying the rawhide on his wrists. The big man coiled the rawhide, turned and went across to the patient. Keeping an eye on him, Turlough worked on the rawhide binding his feet.

'What are you gonna do with me?' he asked again.

'Get that fire going,' was the growled reply. 'I need hot water.'

Rubbing feeling back into his hands, Turlough set about his tasks and brought the water as instructed. He watched as the man washed the other's wounds and then his face. There was tenderness in the action and Turlough was mesmerised as he watched, comparing the brutality of his own treatment to the gentle ministrations now being performed on Milo.

'You're not angry at me anymore?' he asked nervously.

'Make yourself useful and get some coffee going. I could do with something to eat. You'll find coffee and vittles in that sack.'

Turlough scuttled to do as he was bid and soon had coffee brewed. He poured two mugs and took one to his companion who remained watching over Milo. The coffee was received without a word. Turlough went back to the fire and cooked up two plates of fatback and beans.

He sat by the fire eating and keeping a wary eye on his companion, wondering if now would be a good time to make a break for it but also if he would make it to safety before he would be caught and beaten to death. There was a dangerous quality to his jailor that induced nervousness and a fear of provoking him. Turlough ate his meal and brooded on his chances of survival.

He was jerked out of his musing when his companion tossed his empty plate over towards him. Turlough twitched and glanced nervously over his shoulder. The big man was moving towards him and he tensed as he awaited a blow or a kick – like a cowed dog watching its master on the move, regretting now he hadn't made a run for it after all. The big man squatted down beside Turlough, pulled out the makings and began building a smoke.

'Who were they?'

'Huh?'

Those gimlet eyes turned on Turlough and he quailed before their coldness.

'Don't act stupid with me. I've been out there and examined the signs. A bunch of horsemen rode through here searching for someone and I figured that someone was you. So tell me everything about them. If you lie to me I'll rip your arms off.'

Turlough gulped and started to talk.

'I . . . I guess it was all my fault. Clive Carter and his gang were chasing me. I was just running. I didn't even know where I was. Your friend Milo befriended me. Somehow they tracked me down and he ran afoul of them. I saw them beating him and tried to help. I had no weapon so I chucked a rock and hit one of them and they come after me. I hid and they went on. I came back to see if I could help Milo and found him in a pretty bad way. He revived enough to show me how to get to his cave and I brought him in here. I could have taken the money and left but I wouldn't do that.'

'Who is this Carter?'

'Elwood Black's enforcer. Clive Carter is a gunman who does most of his dirty work for him. He's reckoned to be deadly with a gun. No one is his equal.'

'So why were they chasing you?'

Turlough took up a twig and poked at the fire.

'I don't suppose you have tobacco to spare?' he asked.

The big man tossed over his tobacco pouch. Turlough started rolling his smoke. Turlough spilled some tobacco as the other man growled at him.

'Don't stop talking.'

'They said I killed someone,' he mumbled.

'Do I have to beat the information outta you? Who did you kill and why?'

So Turlough told it all.

'My family live in a mining town. We have a claim as do most of the folks around. The biggest mine is Alliance Holdings owned by Elwood Black. Black wants all the mine workings under his control. He offered to buy us out but the price was so low no one took him up. So he sends his hound dog, Carter and his gang to soften us up. They would come into the diggings and ride roughshod over everything, wrecking equipment and setting fire to huts and anything of use. Some people upped and left but most held on.

'One of Carter's sidekicks, Alfie Manning, waylaid my sister and attacked her. I suppose he thought he could do anything he liked just because he was under Carter's protection. I got in a fight with Manning. Afterwards he was found dead and I was accused of killing him. I tried to tell them he was alive when I left him. When Sheriff Ginsberg came after me I had to go on the run.'

Turlough fell silent, thinking over the awful events. He had found his sister with torn clothing and sobbing. He made her tell him who had done it and then he went after Manning. The gang member was bigger than Turlough but in the end proved himself a coward. Brave enough when attacking a young girl, he proved no match against the youngster driven by anger and thoughts of revenge.

'So you're wanted for murder.'

'Yeah, but I didn't do it.'

'If that was so why'd you run?'

'Sheriff Ginsberg said he was gonna hang me for the killing.'

'Why was that if you were innocent?'

'Sheriff Ginsberg is not an impartial officer of the law. He was appointed by Elwood Black, the man who owns the biggest mine in the valley. Ginsberg is the mine owner's man, lock, stock and barrel. Black wanted me dead just as he wants anyone dead who opposes his takeover of the claims.'

'This claim of yours, who's looking after it now?'

'It belonged to Pa but he was killed in a fight with Carter. Ma and me and sis were left to run it. Now there is only Ma and sis and I don't know if sis will be fit to help now she's laid up.'

The men smoked in silence. Turlough stared bleakly into the fire, his thoughts eaten up with bitterness at the hand that fate had dealt him. Without him there to help, he reckoned his ma would have no choice but to sell out to Elwood Black. Through his own foolish actions, he had lost his family as well as their diggings that now their enemies would hijack. There came a low moan from Milo and his companion rose swiftly and knelt by his side.

# 7

'Bring a warm drink,' Turlough was instructed.

It took only moments for the youngster to produce a mug of coffee. Milo's eyes were open and he was looking up at the big man.

'Cyriac, you're back.'

'Don't talk. Have a sup of this.'

Turlough squatted nearby, wondering at the tenderness of the big man who had treated him so brutally. As if he had communicated his thoughts to Milo, he turned his head slightly and saw Turlough squatting nearby.

'Don't hurt the kid. It weren't his fault.'

Every word was gasped out with great effort.

'Hush now, Milo, I ain't hurting nobody excepting those as did this to you.'

'No, don't go near them. I don't need no vengeance for this. They're bad medicine. I don't want you going on a killing spree.'

'You're my brother. They hurt you, they hurt me.'

'I'm done for. Afore I go promise me you'll keep outta trouble.'

'Hell, Milo, you know I can't do that. Trouble just tags along, no matter where I go. You know that. And anyway, I'll pack you on a horse and take you to a sawbones. They'll patch you up.'

'Not this time, Cyriac. Can you light a candle? I'd like to watch the flame for a while. Young 'un, what's your name?'

'Turlough Benedict. I'm sorry you got hurt.'

'Yeah, so am I, son. Was it you as throwed the rock?'

'Yes, sir. I thought it might distract them a mite – I mean, stop them from beating you.'

While Turlough was talking, Cyriac moved away and lit a candle and placed it in a crack in the rock wall.

'You know any prayers, Turlough?' Milo asked.

'Sure, Ma taught them to me. Made me learn them off by heart.'

'Would you mind telling some for me? I never was one for religion and preachifying but now I'm at the end of my days it might do some good if you said some prayers for me.'

Turlough glanced at Cyriac, wondering how he might react to him praying.

'Do as he asks,' came the gruff command.

'OK, I'll do my best.' Turlough paused a moment, thinking, and then launched into a recital. 'Our Father, who art in heaven, help in our time of need: we humbly beseech

31

thee to heal thy sick servant Milo. Look upon him with the eyes of thy mercy; comfort him with a sense of thy goodness; and give him patience under his affliction. In thy good time, restore him to health, and enable him to lead the rest of his life in thy love, and dedicated to thy glory; and grant that finally he may dwell with thee in life everlasting. Amen.'

'Goddamn it, Turlough,' Milo whispered, 'that sure is a fine bit of praying. If that don't set good with them heavenly fellows up there then I don't know what will.' There was a moment of silence before the dying man spoke again. 'Cyriac, would you light that candle now?'

The big man plucked the candle from its niche and held it up in front of his brother.

'Here you are, Milo. It's right here.'

There was no response. Turlough peered into Milo's sick face.

'I . . . think he's gone.'

He heard a moan and the big man had sunk to his knees with his hands across his face. The moaning went on as the bereaved man rocked back and forth. Turlough sat perfectly still, afraid to move in case he sparked off some violent reaction from Cyriac. He cringed as his companion abruptly stood, strode to the cave entrance and disappeared outside. Not having any coin, Turlough searched and found two small pebbles which he placed on the dead man's eyes.

'Rest in peace, Milo. I guess you'd still be alive if I hadn't turned up.'

Still apprehensive of what would happen when Cyriac returned, he pulled a blanket around his shoulders and sat with his back against the wall.

'I don't know if he's gonna blame me for his brother's death and kill me out of hand or just let me go on my way,' he muttered. 'It's like being in the company of a wild bear.'

From somewhere outside there came the sound of shots and Turlough jerked nervously.

'What the hell!'

His first thoughts were that the Carter gang had come back and found Cyriac. He crept to the entrance and peered out. Because of the screen of bushes and trees camouflaging the mouth of the cave, Turlough could see nothing. In order to find out what was going on he would have to venture outside. He turned back and searched for a weapon but there was no sign of the firearms he knew had been there.

'Goddamn it, he's taken all the guns.'

Turlough crept outside and began stalking through the undergrowth. On the way he picked up a broken branch as a possible weapon, thinking it was poor defence against someone with a gun.

He circled around the area, stopping and listening every so often but could see nothing that would explain the shooting. There was a sudden movement and something came winging out of the air towards him. Turlough swung his makeshift weapon and hit a heavy object that nearly wrenched the branch from his hand. He stumbled back and stared in puzzlement at the thing he had clubbed. A good sized turkey was sprawled in the dirt.

'Hell, even the turkeys around here are hostile.' Then he noticed the man standing watching him. 'Cyriac,' Turlough began nervously. 'Was that you?'

The big man raised his hand. Suspended from it was a second turkey.

'You think you could cook these? We're gonna hold a funeral feast. It's what Milo would have wanted.'

For a few moments Turlough studied the man opposite. He bent and picked up the turkey at his feet and handed it to Cyriac.

'You take it back. I got some foraging to do.'

Without waiting for a reply he turned and walked away, wondering if at any moment there would be a shot in his back. But nothing happened and he continued walking.

Turlough knew exactly what he was looking for and when he returned to the cave with his booty stored in his shirt, he was pleasantly surprised to find the birds had been plucked and gutted. He placed his finds on the floor.

'Mushrooms, mustard and watercress to go with the main course and I found some blueberries and raspberries for dessert.'

If he thought he would get a word of praise he was disappointed. Turlough noticed Cyriac had been busy sprucing up his brother. The dead man's hair was neatly brushed and his clothes tidied. The pebbles Turlough had placed on his eyes had been replaced with coins. He said nothing but got on with his cooking.

In a short time he had a brisk fire going and the turkey spitted and roasting. Cyriac produced a full bottle of whiskey which, unlike the dreadful Coffin Varnish variety, was a decent brand appropriately enough named Wild Turkey. He poured generous measures into two mugs and handed one to Turlough.

'To Milo,' he toasted. 'To Milo and to the men who killed him. May they roast in hell.'

And later when Turlough served up the meal, his taciturn companion made another toast.

'A man can do no better thing under the sun than to eat drink and be merry, for tomorrow we will go in search of the men who killed Milo.'

Turlough, more than a little drunk, looked up in surprise.

'The first part of that about eat, drink and be merry is from the Bible,' he said. 'But you must remember it also

34

says: "beloved, never avenge yourselves, but leave it to the wrath of God, for it is written, vengeance is mine, I will repay, says the Lord".'

'Is that what you were thinking when you killed the man who attacked your sister?'

'I told you I didn't kill him. When I parted from him he was still alive. Either someone else killed him or he died from natural causes.'

'The end result was the same,' Cyriac said. 'An eye for an eye; a tooth for a tooth.'

# 8

Next morning Cyriac nudged Turlough awake. 'Get the coffee on,' he ordered. 'I'll be gone awhile.'

Turlough groaned and did not move even after his companion disappeared outside. His head was a dull ache and his stomach felt cramped and there was a nauseous feeling in his gorge. His mouth felt as if it had been stuffed with a rag he had cleaned his boots with.

'I'll never touch another drink,' he moaned.

After a few efforts he made it to his feet and stood swaying, then rushed outside as the queasy feeling in his stomach intensified. When he had finished retching he stood, hands on knees, weak and exhausted. With stumbling steps he made his way down to the stream and dipped his head in the cooling water.

'Never again,' he vowed as he made his way back up to the cave.

35

When Cyriac returned, Turlough had a pot of coffee ready and poured two cups.

'What about breakfast?' Cyriac growled.

'Breakfast – I didn't think you'd want breakfast.'

'For sure we want breakfast. Fella can't travel on an empty belly.'

'You leaving then?' Turlough asked.

Cyriac turned those inexpressive black eyes on the youngster.

'You born with your brain between your legs? What did I tell you last night?'

Turlough tried to get his addled mind to function. He could remember nothing of last night, only a brimming mug of whiskey being handed to him and then another and another.

'Hell, I know what you said,' he mumbled. 'I don't feel too good this morning.'

For reply the big man got up and squatted by the fire where he slung turkey cuts in a pan.

'You need to eat,' he growled. 'Gotta keep your strength up. You got a burying to attend and then we are going on a trip.'

The smell of the cooking meat drove Turlough out into the open again and he tried to be sick but nothing came up.

'God, I feel wretched.'

When he came back inside, Cyriac was tucking into a heaped plate of meat. There were some turkey slices left in the pan but Turlough ignored them and poured himself a mug of coffee. When his plate was empty, Cyriac hooked the pan across and dumped the remainder of the food on his plate and continued eating.

'You ready?' he asked.

Turlough looked up.

'Ready – ready for what?'

Cyriac's eyes narrowed and he shook his head.

'How did you get to be the age you are? We gotta bury Milo and then we go in search of his killers.'

Cyriac wrapped the body in a blanket, lifted the burden like it were nothing but a bedroll and carried it outside with Turlough following. The hole had been dug some distance from the cave. The shovel was standing in the spoil alongside it. Cyriac knelt and gently lowered his dead brother into the grave.

'Say some prayers,' Cyriac growled, staying on his knees with head bowed.

Turlough stood, desperately searching for something to say. Not only was his head throbbing but his brain seemed to have turned to mush.

'Get on with it!'

The harsh command jolted Turlough and out of nowhere came a verse he had heard his mother use when there was a death in the community. He stumbled a bit but remembered most of the words.

'Milo, may the road rise to meet you.
May the wind be always at your back.
May the sun shine warm upon your face,
And the rains fall soft upon your fields.
Until we meet again,
May God hold you in the palm of His Hand.'

For long moments there was no sound in the woods and Turlough stood with head bowed, wondering if the unpredictable man kneeling by his brother's grave expected more from him.

'Amen,' he said at last.

Cyriac stood up and turned towards Turlough. The

37

youngster was startled to see tears running down those scarred cheeks. The big man nodded to him, turned and picked up a handful of dirt and sprinkled it into the grave.

'Farewell, brother. Rest there in peace, knowing that your murderers will soon be joining you in the dirt.'

Hastily Turlough grabbed up a handful of spoil and tossed it into the hole.

'Rest in peace,' he mumbled.

He stood back and watched while Cyriac took the shovel and began filling in the grave. Once the dirt was shovelled in, the big man spent some time chucking leaves and branches on top of the freshly turned soil. When he had finished he stood back and admired his handiwork while wiping his sleeve across his eyes. Abruptly he turned and strode in the direction of the cave with Turlough trailing after. On the way, he retrieved a brace of saddle bags from the inside of a hollow tree.

'We'll have coffee afore we leave.'

As Turlough crouched by the fire and got the brew going, his companion opened his saddle bag and extracted a revolver. It looked very like the Smith & Wesson Turlough had found previously. The big man stood weighing it in his hand, thoughtfully studying Turlough. The youngster's eyes widened.

'Cyriac, please, I swear I had nothing to do with your brother's death,' he pleaded.

'Can you use a gun?'

'Sure I can.'

'Take this.'

He handed the weapon to the youngster and turned away, searching in the saddle bags again. Turlough stared at the gun in his hand. He gripped it firmly and looked across at his companion. Cyriac had his back to him. A wild idea came into Turlough's head, still befuddled by the effects of the alcohol he had consumed last night.

What if he shot the big man and took off with his money and possessions? It looked too easy and Turlough even went so far as to raise the gun and aim it at the broad back presented so temptingly. Then the same qualms that had prevented him from abandoning the wounded Milo stopped him and he turned back to the fire and his coffee preparations. He jumped nervously as a holster and belt landed in the dirt beside him.

'Good job you didn't decide shoot me in the back,' Cyriac commented. 'The gun ain't loaded.'

Turlough looked guiltily at the gun.

'I wouldn't do nothing like that,' he stammered.

'Get yourself ready. We'll be riding out soon.'

'Where are we going?'

'You heard what I promised Milo. We're going after this Black fella and the Carter gang you told me about. The ones as killed him.'

'We can't do that.'

'Can't ain't a word in my vocabulary.'

'You don't understand. To track Carter we gotta go back to Gold Point. As soon as I show up there they'll hang me.'

'The way I see it you got two choices. Either you take me to this Gold Point or I break both your legs and leave you here.'

Which was no choice at all.

Cyriac had two horses corralled downstream of the cave. They retrieved the saddles and got ready to ride out. As Turlough climbed aboard his mount, the big man pointed ahead.

'Seeing as you know the way, you lead. How long do you reckon afore we reach this Gold Point?'

'Depends on how quick you want to get there.'

'We're in no hurry. We'll take our time – spare the horses.'

'Three to four days, then. When I lit out I was on foot so it's hard to guess how far I come. I reckon I was running for the good part of a week. Seems like I didn't run far enough.'

'When trouble stalks a man he can never run far enough,' came the reply.

With deep foreboding Turlough jigged his horse forward. He wanted to protest again against the wisdom of returning to the place where he would be most certainly arrested and then hanged, but he sensed he would be wasting his time appealing to his taciturn companion.

'Damn and blast,' he muttered, 'I'm a dead man no matter what way I turn.'

He put his hand up and massaged his throat as if he could already feel the noose tightening around his neck.

For the most part the pair rode in silence; Turlough brooding on his likely fate at the hands of Sheriff Ginsberg. Cyriac was by nature the strong silent type and answered in monosyllables or not at all if his companion spoke to him. They met no one as they travelled.

The first night they camped in an arroyo. The travellers feasted on beans and fatback which Turlough cooked. After the meal he surreptitiously studied his close-mouthed companion as they sat in silence, smoking and drinking coffee. Noting the scarred and lumpy countenance, he wondered what had caused them but was leery of asking.

Turlough slept well and woke the next morning, and for a time lay where he was, luxuriating in the cosy warmth of his bedroll. Eventually he stretched his limbs and noted his aches and pains seemed to have faded somewhat after a good night's sleep. Carefully he sat up and glanced towards the lightness in the sky.

He felt a strange sense of peace as he observed the big, blue, clear sky merging into a pink vaporous band above the dark mountains. The pink expanded and pulsed, radiating streaks of fire and the sun emerged, orange and radiant. For a brief moment, lost in the beauty of the dawn, he forgot his worries and fears. Then hunger pains brought him back to reality, and Turlough arose and got a fire going.

When his companion awakened, he slid from his blankets smoothly like a serpent emerging from its lair. Turlough noted the big man was clutching his revolver and realized that was how Cyriac slept – with his weapon ready to hand.

Cyriac stretched mightily, standing on tiptoe and reaching towards the dawn tinted sky, a menacing and powerful figure, then he hunkered down beside the fire. Turlough ventured 'good morning' and received a grunt in reply.

The morning ritual continued in silence. Coffee, breakfast and then cleaning up afterwards, all of it done by Turlough. Though he hated to admit it, Cyriac took good care of the horses, looking after Turlough's mount as well as his own. Saddling and unsaddling, rubbing down and feeding and watering and for that at least, Turlough was grateful.

It was another uneventful day and that night they camped by a creek that Turlough recognized. Even this far downstream they could see the damage done by the mining operations at Gold Point.

'Half a day's ride at most and then we're there,' he informed Cyriac, getting the usual grunt in reply.

Once they had set up camp, Cyriac stepped to the water's edge, stripped off his clothes and waded into the creek. Turlough watched while he vigorously soaped and washed himself. At one stage he looked up and noticed Turlough staring at him.

'Get in here and wash,' he growled. 'You stink like a buffalo's cojones.'

'I stink!' Turlough bridled. 'What the hell! I've been on the run for days and then I fell in a goddamn swamp. Is it any wonder I smell?'

Moodily he turned his back on the water and stared into the fire, listening to the splashing coming from behind him. There was a moment of quiet as Cyriac came out, then Turlough felt himself picked up bodily and heaved into the air. He was yelling something incomprehensible before he hit the water face down and went under. Spluttering and trashing about, he came to the surface.

'You goddamn maniac!' he yelled and splashed to the shore, cursing under his breath.

Cyriac was standing towelling himself dry as Turlough crawled on to dry land. He glared at the big man and was about to yell some more abuse when he noticed the scars on Cyriac's body and abruptly thought better of it.

Surreptitiously he noted the small round marks that were probably healed up bullet wounds. There were also puckered seams running at various places – one across the abdomen, two crisscrossing his chest. A long ragged scar ran down the length of one thigh. Smaller marks might have been healed up knife wounds. Turlough looked away and went and huddled by the fire.

'Get them wet clothes off and dry out,' Cyriac growled.

At first Turlough was inclined to tell his companion

42

where to go but then thought better of it when he felt the chill eat into him. With difficulty he undressed, wringing out his garments and placing them by the fire. The soap hit him on the chest, making him jump.

'Get back in there and wash.'

In a fit of pique Turlough picked up the soap and flung it back. Cyriac easily plucked it out of the air.

'Goddamn you! I ain't no goddamn kid you can order around like you was my pa,' he raged. 'You hit me, punch me, near strangle me and then throw me in the creek. I've had enough. I ain't going back to Gold Point. You can do what the hell you like. This is the parting of the ways between you and me.'

He stood stark naked, glaring defiantly at his companion. Cyriac was tossing the soap from one hand to the other, watching him. A slow lopsided grin spread across that scarred countenance.

'So you do have some grit after all. I was wondering how spineless you really were and if you made up that tale about fighting the fella as attacked your sister.' He walked across and handed the soap over. 'To soap or not to soap, that is the question. I got some spare clothes you can wear while yourn are drying out.'

Turlough stood, his mouth agape as he stared from the soap to his companion. Abruptly he shut his mouth, walked to the creek, stepped into the water and began to wash. He came back out shivering and dried himself on a damp piece of cotton and dressed in the clothes Cyriac had left out for him. They were a surprisingly good fit and then he noticed they were brand new.

'How come you got these duds?' he asked.

'I got them for Milo. We planned a trip to Europe and I bought them in anticipation. Only Milo never got to go. Milo always was a dreamer. Wanted to travel and visit the seat of civilization, he said. We were to go to England, France, Spain and then Greece where our folk originally come from.'

Turlough did not know how to respond. He squatted beside the fire and not for the first time had to revise his opinion regarding his gruff companion. At one stage as they ate breakfast, Cyriac asked Turlough if his ma and sister were good cooks.

'Yeah, fair, I would say Ma was pretty durned good. Bakes bread and cakes, too.'

'I'm looking forward to some home cooking. How far is it now?'

Turlough's brow creased as he thought about it.

'I reckon we should get a mite closer later today. But like I keep trying to tell you, I am probably riding towards a necktie party.'

'In that case, the sooner we get started the better.'

# 10

Gold Point hadn't changed much since Turlough had last seen it. Scattered claims littered the valley, creating an untidy mess of dug up dirt and heaps of spoil. This disturbance of the earth, along with the untidy sprawl of crude shelters, gave the place the air of a refugee camp. Tents and crude wooden cabins hastily nailed together and even dugouts clung to whatever space available. And through it all meandered the ancient stream that provided potable water and a medium for washing the dirt and spoilage that

44

the ever optimistic miners spent their days digging out of the rocky soil.

Many thousands of years ago when the land was covered in ice, a glacier had driven down through the rocky valley, deepening and shaping it into the typical U shape of glacial erosion. As the climate warmed and the ice melted, it deposited rocks large and small throughout its course.

Back in 1873, a man called Thomas Edmondson had found a nugget of gold while panning in the valley and as the news leaked out, it started a rush of would-be miners. They came in a continuous stream and settled until the money or credit or hope gave out and they either drifted on to the next dream or settled in or near the town of Thomaston, named after the man who had started it by unearthing that lucky gold nugget.

Turlough and Cyriac rode through the valley, their passage creating idle curiosity as the inhabitants paused in their activities to briefly watch the newcomers.

Men worked at their claims, digging and panning the dirt. Women could be seen at the crude shelters, hanging out washing or supervising the children playing amongst the disorder of the settlement and in some cases, working with the men at the diggings.

Gold Point was a place of clutter and disorder and industry. As soon as the riders passed, the miners went back to their excavating and pan washing and scouring the dirt of the valley for a hint of colour that would change their lives for the better.

Turlough threaded his way through the camp, thinking nothing much had changed during his absence. But then it had only been a matter of days since he went on the run from the law. The tumbledown shack he called home came into sight and he was heartened to see smoke drifting from the chimney. He turned in the saddle and pointed.

45

'That's our place.'

The horses rattled to a halt and Turlough slid from the saddle, conscious of the gun hanging on his side. He turned and nodded to Cyriac who made no response but by now Turlough did not expect any. He pulled off his hat, pushed open the door and stepped inside.

'Ma, I'm back.'

The woman kneading a batch of bread dough turned and Turlough stood with his mouth open.

'I . . . where's Ma, I mean Mrs Benedict?'

She was young and pretty and had a smudge of flour on her chin, and Turlough had never seen anything so enchanting in his short life.

'You . . . I. . . .' Turlough spluttered to a stop.

The girl was frowning at him. 'Who are you?' she asked.

'Turlough Benedict; I live here.'

'Oh, we didn't know. We just moved in. The place was empty.'

They stood staring helplessly at each other, not quite knowing how to proceed. Behind Turlough, the door creaked open and Cyriac stepped inside. As he spied the young woman he took off his hat and grunted.

'Something's happened,' Turlough said. 'Ma and sis ain't here. She says the place was empty when she moved in.'

'You sure you got the right place?' Cyriac growled.

'Course I'm sure. This was my home. I helped build it.'

'Humph! Better ask around. Find out what happened.'

Cyriac stared at Turlough until he could stand it no more and the youngster nodded to the young woman and went back outside. Left alone with Cyriac, the woman watched him, nervously noting his scarred countenance.

'Would you like some coffee while you are waiting?' she asked timidly.

46

'That would be mighty welcome, miss,' Cyriac replied, seating himself on a wooden bench against one wall. 'But don't let me stop you baking. I've heard it said that bread is the staff of life.'

'That's all right; it won't take but a moment to make the coffee. The kettle is boiled already.'

'Are you two related?' she asked as she busied herself pouring hot water into the coffee pot.

'Nope.'

'Just friends then?'

'Nope.'

'We're from Denver,' she said, desperate for some subject that might engage this close-mouthed man. 'Where have you come from?'

He made no reply and she sneaked a glance at him. He was sitting straight-backed, staring at nothing. She went back to her bread making while she waited for the coffee to brew but all the time conscious of his presence, stiff and as unyielding as one of the wooden Indians she had seen standing outside cigar stores in some of the towns they had passed through. The door opened and a large gangly individual stepped inside, decked out in overalls and a battered, misshapen hat.

'What the hell's going on here? We found this place empty and squatted in here so we have squatters' rights. Get your mangy butt outta here afore you're thrown out.'

'Aimee, please,' the young girl pleaded. 'We don't want any trouble.'

Turlough poked his head inside. 'Cyriac, can I have a word?'

'This young lady kindly offered me a coffee and I was just waiting for her to serve it up. Why don't you join me?'

'Cropped mule skins, did you not hear what I said?' Aimee snarled. 'Get the hell outta here while you can still walk under your own steam.'

'Aimee!' The young woman stepped over and took the other by the hand. 'Can we just sit down and discuss this friendly like over a mug of coffee?'

Aimee was big and ornery and she had a scowl on her that would have turned milk sour but she calmed down under the pleading of the younger woman.

'Goddamn it, all right, but we ain't moving outta here. I know my rights.'

Turlough was still hanging by the door as if he was ready to skedaddle back outside again. Cyriac raised his finger and beckoned. Turlough came meekly across and stood with his hat in hand.

'It's bad, Cyriac. Sis is dead and Ma moved on. Some reckon she went into Thomaston. I gotta go in there and find her. But you know what'll happen if I go into town.'

For long moments no one spoke after Turlough had blurted out his news. Then the young woman came across to him and laid her hand on his arm.

'I'm sorry. Won't you sit a while and have a drink? Maybe things aren't as bad as you think.'

Turlough made no resistance as she led him to a chair. Aimee stood indecisive until the younger woman also took her hand.

'Sit down, Aimee. Let's do this civilized.'

The big woman scowled and stomped over to the opposite wall to stand glowering at Cyriac and Turlough.

'Nobody speak until I have served up the coffee,' the younger woman admonished. 'Then we will introduce ourselves and everyone will get a chance to talk.'

There was silence as she set about the task of pouring the coffee, serving the guests first and then Aimee and finally herself.

'Now we can begin.'

# 11

'My name is Beth Rawlinson and this is my sister or rather, half-sister, Aimee. We arrived here a few days ago and found this place empty. We had no idea it belonged to anyone. I'm sorry about your family. I know what it is like to lose someone close.'

Turlough nodded dumbly, too sunk in misery to speak and the introductions were left to Cyriac.

'Cyriac Halkias, Miss Rawlinson, and this here is Turlough Benedict. Seems to me, this is between you and Turlough here. How you resolve it is up to you. The first thing is to find his ma and take her opinion into consideration. Perhaps she'll not want to come back again on account it might have too many bad memories.'

'Why don't we share until things shake out?' Beth suggested. 'I would be agreeable to that.'

She looked questionably at Turlough. He was sitting hunched up in his chair, staring into his coffee.

'The place was empty when we got here,' Aimee growled, scowling across at Cyriac. 'Don't see any reason for sharing.'

An awkward silence followed, broken by Beth.

'I'm preparing supper and I would like you to join us. There's nothing like eating a meal together for making folk amiable. While you are waiting, why don't you have a scout around the camp and see if anyone can tell you more about your family and you can have a think on what you want to do.'

Both men agreed and left. Cyriac separated from

49

Turlough and carried out his own investigation and learned that Lily Benedict, Turlough's sister, was found one morning face down in the river. Then Cyriac made the acquaintance of Gerald Hanley who proclaimed to be a friend of the Benedict family. He spoke frankly of his suspicions regarding the drowning.

'She was knocked about when we found her. I know folks might say she got injured when she fell in the water but I reckon there was a lot of bruising and cuts when we pulled her out.'

'How do you mean?'

'I don't like to speculate, but maybe there was more to her drowning than folk were putting about. If I were you I'd have a word with Doc McCullough. He's the sawbones and the coroner with offices in Thomaston. He might be able to tell you more.'

Cyriac drifted back to the cabin where inside he had to endure the hostile gaze of Aimee and came to the conclusion it was maybe her habitual expression. Certainly he had seen no traces of friendliness from the big woman. He sat stoically, ignoring her. Eventually Turlough came back and strutted inside, smelling heavily of whiskey.

'Nobody knows nothing,' he stated. 'They think Ma might have gone into town but no one knows for sure.'

He slurred his words and stood swaying in the middle of the floor.

'You're drunk,' Aimee snarled. 'Your family go missing and you guzzle moonshine to celebrate. Typical bloody man.'

Turlough tried to focus on his abuser.

'Not only are you ugly but you're ornery to boot.'

'You sad excuse for a man. Your ma you claim to be so fond of did herself no favours when she didn't drown you at birth.'

'Don't you slander my ma.'

Turlough took a step towards the woman, his hands clenched. Whatever his intentions were, he never got a chance to execute them. Aimee moved swiftly and hooked his feet from under him. Turlough went down like a felled steer with Aimee straddling him.

'You want to fight!' she yelled, slapping the youth's face. 'I'll rip your bloody arm off and stick it up your butt.'

'Aimee!' Beth called. 'For God's sake, don't disgrace us brawling like a barroom harpy.'

The smaller woman was hauling on Aimee's arm with little or no effect other than preventing her from slapping Turlough again. Aimee scowled at her sister but came reluctantly to her feet. As she was pulled back, she could not resist lashing out at Turlough with her boot. He mumbled drunkenly and curled into a ball. Beth was persistent – pushing her much bigger sister towards a chair.

'Sit there and don't move. Supper is nearly ready.' She turned to Cyriac who had sat quietly observing the fracas. 'And you weren't much use. Can you not keep your friend under control?'

'He ain't no friend of mine. I just happen to be travelling with him. He sure as hell can't hold his liquor.'

Beth put her fists on her hips and stood glaring at her companions one by one.

'All of you behave,' she ordered sternly. 'Anyone steps out of line again gets no supper.'

No one responded. Cyriac went back to being his usual stoic self. Aimee glowered while Turlough slowly sat up and sent sullen glances at her. The smell of cooking filled the cabin and had a calming effect on the inhabitants, for there were no more disagreements. A truce was in place and for the moment all was quiet while the cook got on with the task of producing the meal.

The foursome sat down to braised beef and potatoes. No one spoke much until Cyriac broached the subject of Turlough's family.

'From what I can gather your sister was found drowned. And it is probable when your ma lost so many members of her family she upped and left. I can't say I blame her. No one knows where she went but I guess Thomaston would be a good place to start.'

'I told you what'll happen if I go into Thomaston. Sheriff Ginsberg has a noose he's saving for me. I don't feel like putting my head in it any time soon.'

'Don't surprise me they want to hang you,' Aimee sneered. 'You're like a mangy dog no one wants.'

'Would you like me to go in for you?' Beth asked hastily, trying to stave off more disagreements.

Turlough looked across at Beth with surprise. 'You would do that for me?'

'It's not much to ask,' she said. 'I'll go in first thing in the morning.'

'Typical man,' Aimee sneered. 'Can't do his own dirty work. Got to get a female to help him out. Not only are you a lush but a coward to boot.'

'Aimee, that's not fair,' Beth remonstrated with her sister. She turned back to Turlough. 'What makes you think you are in danger from the sheriff?'

Turlough had eaten very little of his dinner, pushing it around the plate. Cyriac reached over, took the plate and swapped it for his own empty one.

'What the hell you do that for?' protested Turlough.

'If I remember right, the last time you had a bellyful of whiskey you couldn't eat anything. I'm just saving you the embarrassment of leaving this excellent dinner on the plate and humiliating the cook.'

'Damn you, you've gone too far this time.' Turlough

staggered to his feet.

Ignoring the outburst, Cyriac continued eating.

'You cook a mighty fine beef, Miss Beth,' he said as he chewed. 'He'll be a lucky man as throws a loop on you and gets you to the altar. Sit down, Turlough. You are embarrassing everyone as well as making a fool of yourself. Is that any way to thank someone as feeds you and then offers to go into town to help you out?'

Turlough sat down abruptly. 'Sorry, miss,' he mumbled.

'Tell you what,' Cyriac continued. 'How about we all go into town tomorrow and enquire about your family?'

'Huh!' snorted Aimee. 'You can count me out. I ain't going into no town with no gallows bait. If he says as the sheriff wants to hang him I'd more 'an likely give him a hand.'

'That's settled then.' Cyriac poured the last of the gravy on Turlough's purloined dinner. 'We can all go in and watch the hanging.'

He glanced over at his companion. Turlough was slumped in the chair, fast asleep.

## 12

Aimee decided after all to accompany them into town. 'If this jerk is gonna be hanged I want to be there to help,' she averred.

She rode a sturdy Belgian sorrel while Beth, in keeping with her own neat shape, had saddled up a compact Mustang. Turlough was slumped on his mount, looking pale and washed out. Cyriac was his usual impassive self.

Beth tried to draw out Turlough on his family but the youngster was too sunk in his own misery and fear of what was to come that he was unable to engage with her and thereafter the quartet travelled in silence.

The town of Thomaston was composed of hastily erected buildings and shacks. The main street was wide and muddy with a few shoddy attempts at boardwalks here and there. It was a settlement that had grown up overnight with the appearance that it might vanish just as quickly. They pulled up just on the outskirts.

'How do you want to do this?' Beth deferred to Cyriac.

'Best we split up. I'll mosey along to the sawbones. I was told he is the coroner.'

Without waiting for a response, he urged his mount forward, leaving them to gaze after him, undecided.

'I guess you'll make your enquiries in the saloon,' Aimee mocked Turlough. 'You have plenty of choice. There's three to choose from.'

Turlough pulled his hat low on his face and rode down the street, following behind the sisters.

Cyriac saw the sign outside the clapboard house, proclaiming it was the residence of Doctor McCullough MD. He tied up his horse outside and knocked. A young woman opened the door to him and welcomed him inside.

'What can I do for you?'

'I need to see the doc.'

'Take a seat.' She pointed to a bench. 'Doctor McCullough is with someone at the moment. What is your name?'

'Halkias.'

The woman disappeared through a door off the hallway. Within minutes she reappeared with a coffee tray and placed it on a small table beside him. Cyriac nodded appreciatively and poured himself a coffee, thinking the woman was very young to be a doctor's wife and a hell of an attractive one at that.

He drank one cup and was contemplating pouring himself another when the door opened and a chubby matron came out into the corridor. She ignored Cyriac and left by the front door. The young woman came into the hall again.

'Mr Halkias, Doctor McCullough will see you now.'

Cyriac was surprised to discover the doctor was an elderly man with sparse hair and a drooping grey moustache. He realized the error of his first guess that the young woman was the doctor's wife and concluded she had to be his daughter.

'What can I do for you?' the doctor asked.

'I'm after some information about a young woman as drowned recently out at Gold Point. Name of Lily Benedict.'

The doctor squinted at him. 'You a relative?'

'No, but I'm here on behalf of her brother, Turlough Benedict.'

'Mmm . . . there ain't much to tell. She fell in the water and drowned.'

'The fella as found her tells me she was badly knocked about. He wondered if there was foul play. Said as you were the coroner you would be able to tell me more.'

The doctor turned his gaze away from Cyriac. 'I can't tell you any more than I just did, mister. Either way it's hard to say if it was suicide or an accident.'

Cyriac sensed there was more and wondered if it was worth pursuing the matter but decided against it. He got a sense from the interview the doctor was reluctant to say anything more.

'A young girl dies and no one gives a damn. Thank you, Doc.'

As he rose to go he heard someone at the front door. After a pause there was a sudden scuffle and he heard a woman cry out. Doctor McCullough came out of his chair and pushed past Cyriac.

'What the hell are you doing, Linenan?' he yelled once he was in the hall. 'Get the hell outta my house at once.'

'Sure, Doc, as soon as this little filly of yours starts treating me with some respect. I came here asking to walk her out and you slammed the door in my face.'

'Leave me alone, you brute. I wouldn't walk out with you if you were the last man on earth,' came a woman's voice.

The intruder was almost as big as Cyriac. His face was red; suffused either with rotgut or rage or both. The doctor's daughter was feisty all right, even though Linenan had her pinned against the wall, his hands roaming over her like he had every right, while she struggled futilely against his greater strength.

'You get out of here at once,' the doctor yelled. 'Else I'll put a charge of buckshot in you.'

The big man's face turned to the doctor. He placed his hand on the butt of the six gun strapped to his side.

'You figure on swapping lead with me, Doc. Go ahead. Get your scattergun. See which of us is standing at the end of the shootout.'

Holding on to the woman's wrist, he stepped a pace back from her.

'You're drunk,' the doctor raged. 'Get the hell away from here and come back when you're sober.'

The outer door opened and another man stepped in, not quite as big as Linenan but bulky with muscle.

'You having problems, Jesse?' he asked.

'Nothing I can't handle,' answered Linenan. 'The doc

here wants to have a shootout with me. What way's that to behave just because a fella comes a-courting?' He leered at his captive. 'What's it to be, Arlene? You gonna behave yourself and come along with me for a sociable drink or will your pa and me have a good old-fashioned shooting match?'

The intruders either didn't notice Cyriac standing in the background or chose to ignore him. Now he stepped along the hallway.

'Miss McCullough can't come with you. She has a prior engagement with me.'

Linenan's eyes narrowed. Slowly he turned and it was only then Cyriac saw the star on his chest.

'Mister, I'd advise you to go on about your business and not interfere in this. You're a stranger around here and obviously don't know how things work in Thomaston. I'll give you a piece of friendly advice cos I'm a friendly sorta fella. You go back in doc's office and wait for him to attend you, or you keep interfering and when Trent and me here have finished working you over, even the doc won't be able to patch you up. Then again, seeing as I'm in an easy going mood, I might just take you down the calaboose and sling you in jail for disturbing the peace. You and doc go back to your business, and me and Arlene here will go down the Golden Garter for a friendly drink.'

Cyriac threw his hands wide on either side, palms out.

'I see you got a badge. I didn't realize you were the law. I guess I'll mosey along then.'

He stepped past the doctor. Linenan was smirking as he watched the big man move along the hallway.

'Smart move, mister.'

As Cyriac drew near the couple, he doffed his hat with his left hand and nodded towards the young woman.

'Good day, miss.'

He jammed the hat in Linenan's face and at the same

time, his hand snaked out and snatched the gun from the lawman's holster. Linenan gasped out loud as the gun was rammed hard into his midriff. There was a click sounding loud in that hallway as Cyriac pulled the trigger.

'You crazy son of a bitch,' Linenan whispered, his voice trembling, 'you could have shot me then.'

'You were lucky that time, fella. Most folk as carry a gun keep the first chamber empty. I couldn't be sure but then I didn't care anyway. So I guess the pin is now resting on a live shell. When next I pull the trigger, you'll get a lead ball in your guts. Miss, you go on back there and join your pa. I wouldn't want you to get this fella's blood over you.'

Hastily the young woman moved out of danger.

'It's my turn to give a piece of friendly advice,' Cyriac continued. 'You can turn and walk out that door under your own steam or I can pull this trigger and maybe the doc here can save your life or then again, maybe not. I wouldn't count on him being too anxious to patch you up seeing as you're not on very friendly terms at the moment.' The silence was tangible in the hallway until Cyriac spoke again. 'If your pal by the door doesn't take his hand away from that gun then he'll join you on the casualty list.'

Jesse Linenan, deputy to Sheriff Ginsberg, looked into those dark eyes and thought he saw his own death in the depths.

'I'll go,' he croaked.

Cyriac stuffed the purloined revolver in his belt and watched impassively as the two men scrambled out of the door.

# 13

The sheriff's office was situated halfway along the main thoroughfare. A few boards had been thrown down to keep the mud tramping inside to a minimum, though during the rainy season it rarely worked.

The town drunk – a shabbily dressed man wearing an old peaked cap rusty with age – stomped a few times on the boards and then pushed open the door to the law office. Inside he found two men playing cards.

'Sheriff Ginsberg,' he wheezed as if he had lung trouble. 'I need to see the sheriff.'

'Gusty, get outta here. Sheriff ain't in today.'

'You gotta tell me where he is at. I got something urgent to tell him.'

'Did someone steal a nickel from you?' teased one, a weasel-faced man with a drooping moustache covering most of his mean mouth.

'Just go back to lying in the gutter,' his partner said. 'You look outta place standing upright.'

The second man was the opposite of the first – bulging out of his vest and with a ruddy rounded face. Gusty was not to be put off by the banter.

'You don't understand. It's real important as I see the sheriff.'

'Gusty, I tell you he ain't here,' the first man said impatiently. 'Now get outta here afore I kick your sorry butt back out into the street. I raise you a nickel,' he said to his partner, chucking money into the small heap of coins on the desk.

'Mmm. . . .' The tubby man studied his cards with a frown, wrinkling his forehead.

'It's Turlough Benedict,' Gusty burst out, unable to contain his news any longer. 'He's back in town. I saw him.'

That got the attention of the two deputies.

'Benedict – are you sure? He wouldn't show his face back here again. He wouldn't dare.'

'I tell you I seen him.' Gusty was hopping up and down in his excitement. 'He got some females with him. I saw him go in the store. He was asking about his ma.'

'Well, I'll be danged. You sure it was Benedict?'

' 'Course I'm sure. I know Benedict from when he useta come in the Golden Garter. Time or two he bought me a drink.'

The deputies looked at each other, frowning.

'What you think, Nick? Should we go get him?'

'Hell, Duran, he's a killer. Maybe we should wait for back up.'

'Yeah, you're right. Where's Linenan? He should be around.'

'He's visiting the sawbones. He's took a shine to the doc's daughter.'

'Gusty, run and fetch Linenan. Tell him he's needed urgently back here.'

'Sure thing.' The barfly was eying the money on the desk. 'Thirsty work all this running around,' he said, licking his lips.

'Hell, you'll get your drink when we pull in Benedict and not afore.'

Muttering about the meanness of deputies, the old man left on his errand. As it was, he did not have to go all the way to the doc's place but met the two deputies partway there.

'Say,' he began, 'I was just on my way to fetch you.'

60

That was as far as he got before Linenan punched him, sending the old man into the dirt.

'Outta my way, slush head,' he snarled and aimed a kick at the fallen man.

Gusty was squealing and scrambling away from the deputy on hands and knees, but Linenan went after the drunkard, wanting to take his anger out on someone weaker than himself. His companion pulled him back.

'Jesse, leave the old sponger alone. He ain't worth it.'

Snarling with rage, Linenan allowed Trent to pull him away.

'Let's go and have a drink. We can waylay that drifter anytime and sling him in jail for assaulting a lawman. We might even get to hang him. You know how fond Ginsberg is of hanging.'

'Who is he anyway? I ain't ever seen him afore.'

'No matter, he'll get his comeuppance.'

Back at the jailhouse, the two deputies waited for their fellow officers.

'Damn that old soak, he's probably forgotten what we sent him out for. We'll go ourselves and fetch Linenan.'

As they stepped into the street they spotted Jesse Linenan and Trent Masterson approaching.

'What's up?' Linenan called.

'We spotted Turlough Benedict. We were waiting for you so we can go get him.'

'Benedict! That son of a bitch come back? What are you waiting for? Let's go get him.'

'Where's he at?'

'He was seen going in the store. We'll try there first.'

Linenan slapped his empty holster. 'Hell, I ain't got no gun. Wait there.'

He disappeared into the jailhouse to reappear moments

later with a Smith & Wesson, spinning the chamber to make sure it was fully loaded.

'Let's go get that murdering son of a bitch.'

The lawmen stalked down the street, hands on gun butts.


Turlough's enquiries at the store didn't bring him any nearer to finding out where his mother had gone. The storekeeper remembered her attending her daughter's funeral but after that she seemed to have dropped out of sight.

'Maybe she went back to her folks,' the storekeeper suggested. 'With her family gone there was nothing here for her.'

But Turlough was not satisfied. Surely his mother would have waited for some news of him before departing Gold Point. It didn't make sense.

'Ma wouldn't have gone off like that without leaving word,' he confided to Beth. 'I'm worried something happened to her. Black's men have been harassing folk at Gold Point to make them give up their claims so he can take them over. He wants the whole diggings to himself and he won't stop until he gets it by fair means or foul.'

'I'm sure there's a simple explanation for her not being here,' Beth tried to reassure him. 'Maybe she wanted a break from the place for a spell. She's lost her son and then her daughter so she probably went somewhere to get over it. Somewhere that wouldn't remind her of her loss.'

'If I had a no-account brat for a son I would've taken off, too,' was Aimee's contribution.

'Well, that'll never happen as no man would ever look twice at you, never mind want a kid with you.'

They glowered at each other.

'I'll go down to the saloon and make enquiries there,'

Turlough suggested in an effort to get away from Aimee's persistent heckling.

'Oh yeah, the only enquiries you'll be doing is into how many shots of redeye in a bottle.'

'It was a woeful day you sneaked into my home, Aimee Rawlinson,' was Turlough's parting shot.

He stepped outside and saw the deputies waiting for him in the road.

'Benedict! How nice of you to give yourself up,' Linenan crowed.

Turlough stared with growing apprehension at the line of lawmen.

'Are you gonna come quietly or do I have to pistol-whip you like you deserve?' the deputy called.

Beth, hearing the voices came outside. 'What's this about?' she demanded.

'Keep outta this, missy. That excuse for a man there is a murdering hound and we're here to arrest him. I personally am looking forward to hanging him.'

'The way I heard it he was protecting his sister. That doesn't stack up to murder by any account.'

'Hell, I ain't got time to argue with no sassy hussy.'

The deputies closed in on Turlough, who backed against the store front. Beth was helpless as she was brushed aside. Linenan pulled his gun and swiped the unfortunate youth across the head. Turlough sagged against the wall. Again the deputy hit out and the youngster's knees gave way. As he toppled the lawman kneed him in the face. Turlough collapsed, groaning. Blood trickled down his face from the gash in his head.

'There's no need to beat him,' Beth protested.

Aimee grabbed her and pulled her back.

'Leave it, sis. He got what he deserved. He's a murderer.'

Beth watched helplessly as the lawmen took an arm apiece and dragged Turlough towards the jailhouse.

'Oh,' she moaned, 'what'll happen to him?'

'What he deserves – a hanging!' was all the sympathy she got from her acerbic sister.

# 14

Cyriac stood in the doorway watching the two lawmen until they were out of sight. He turned back to the doctor and his daughter.

'They've gone,' he said simply. 'I'll go, too.'

Doc McCullough moved forward and taking Cyriac's arm, tugged him inside before closing the door.

'That's Jesse Linenan you just buffaloed. He is deputy to Sheriff Ginsberg. A meaner gang of unnatural villains that ever walked – with Ginsberg himself the meanest. And all under the shield of the law. God help the poor people of Thomaston that have such a carbuncle imposed upon them. I'm afraid you've laid up a mite of trouble for yourself, Mr Halkias.'

'Trouble! I can't remember a time when I wasn't in trouble.'

Looking at the big man's scarred countenance, the doctor could well believe it.

'You've seen how they behave. Walking into a man's home and molesting his womenfolk. Because they wear a badge they believe they're above the law. My advice to you is to leave this area. They're such a crowd of hell-kites they won't rest until they've got their revenge. And that don't exclude a cowardly shooting in the back.'

'Well, thanks for the warning, Doc, I'll bear that in mind.'

'Arlene, get the whiskey bottle. Mr Halkias and me have some talking to do.' The doctor ushered Cyriac along the hallway and into a parlour. 'Make yourself comfortable. I'll tell you what you want to know.'

Arlene came in carrying a tray with a decanter and glasses. She poured the drinks including one for herself and offered a jug of water to the men which Cyriac refused, preferring his whiskey neat. She fixed her own drink and sat down.

'I want to thank you for rescuing me from that brute,' she said.

Cyriac did not answer and sipped his drink. He was conscious of the young woman opposite studying him but kept his attention on Doctor McCullough.

'You came in here asking about the Benedict girl,' the doctor said. 'I wasn't quite straight with you. I'm the coroner for the area, and the girl was brought in to me and I examined her. I found bruising and injuries on her body which made me suspicious. I probed a little deeper and I established there was no water in her lungs. Which means she was dead afore entering the water.

'When I informed Sheriff Ginsberg of my findings he told me not to pursue it. I tried to take it further but he told me some very important people were not too pleased with me, and any further probing into the Benedict girl's death would get me in trouble. I suspect today's little fracas with Linenan was a taste of what I would expect if I didn't do as I was told.' The doctor took a sip of his drink before concluding, 'That's the long and short of it.'

'I take it this is all to do with the mining at Gold Point.'

'That's precisely what it's all about. There's people here as want the whole shebang under their control. They want to mine on an industrial scale and make a killing. There's a steady harassment of anybody with a claim. The least misdemeanour by a miner and they're slung in jail and heavily fined. They come into town and you can be sure some of the sheriff's men are at them – hassling and taunting them until they can't take it no more and they snap back. That gives the deputies an excuse to pistol-whip them and they are then dragged off to a cell. Some are lingering in jail for weeks because they can't find the money to pay off Ginsberg.

'And they are the lucky ones. Sometimes it explodes into gunplay and the miner is gunned down. I've lost count of the number of miners I've seen buried. I know mining towns have a reputation for violence but Thomaston sure beats them all into a hard hat.'

'In the name of the law,' Cyriac murmured.

'As you say, in the name of the law. So now you know what we are up against, are you going to heed my warning and leave Thomaston for a healthier climate?'

'Thank you for your counsel, Doctor. I have some business to take care of afore I can move on.'

'You said you were acting on behalf of Turlough Benedict. What is your connection with the family if you don't mind me asking?'

'My brother asked me to take care of him. I feel obliged.' Cyriac drained his glass. 'I thank you for telling me how the land lies. And thank you for the whiskey.'

He turned and in doing so, caught the eye of Arlene. She was staring at him so intently he dropped his eyes immediately.

'I gotta go now.'

He stood and put his glass on a low table. He suddenly

felt big and awkward in that elegant parlour.

'Won't you stay for dinner, Mr Halkias?' Arlene asked.

'I sure would love to, miss, but I have some pressing business to attend to.'

But Arlene was not to be put off so easily. She was intrigued by this big man whose face bore the scars of past and violent conflicts. He had come to her rescue even though he had been under no obligation to do so. She and her father were complete strangers yet he had not hesitated to put himself in danger. In spite of his rough appearance she sensed that here was a man of strength and principle and honour.

'Then this evening you will come to supper,' she averred. 'I shall expect you at six o'clock.'

Cyriac stared helplessly at her and was at a loss.

'Miss,' he muttered and turned to go, fumbling with the door handle and then exiting.

They heard the front door close. Doctor McCullough was watching his daughter.

'What was that about?' he asked.

'I just wanted to thank him for helping us,' she said and massaged her wrist where Linenan had gripped it. 'And he interests me.'

'Careful, Arlene, you've never shown interest in anyone since Robert.'

'I know, Father. Robert was another victim of the violence that plagues Gold Point.'

'Maybe we should pack up and leave. Thomaston has too many bad memories for you.'

'That man there that just left. Maybe Elwood Black and his hired killers are messing with someone who might just be too much for them to handle.'

'I wouldn't count on it. Black has a lot of bad hats around him. Halkias is but one man. My guess he'll do whatever he came here to do and then move on. Men like that never stay in one place for long.'

'Cyriac Halkias,' Arlene said. 'That sounds like a Greek name. Maybe the blood of Greek heroes runs in his veins. Who shall we liken him to, Father? Achilles!'

McCullough was shaking his head in perplexity.

'You always were a dreamer, Arlene. Just like your mother. I never saw a more unlikely hero. His face bears the marks of dozens of battles. For all we know he might be here to join up with Elwood Black and his bully boys.'

'I don't think so, somehow. There's more to Cyriac Halkias than meets the eye.'

'Time will tell, my dear,' the doctor said. 'Do you think he'll accept your invitation to supper?'

Arlene smiled.

'Oh, he'll come all right. I'm sure of that.'

# 15

Cyriac could see the horses tied up outside the store and figured that was a good place to enquire where his companions had got to. He was pleased to find he did not have to go looking as the two females were inside, drinking coffee served up by the storekeeper who kept a separate part of his store as an eating joint.

'Oh, Mr Halkias, am I glad to see you,' Beth said, standing up and wringing her hands in her agitation.

Cyriac called for a coffee and sat down at the table. 'What's up?'

'That lame dog you brought back with you is in jail,' gloated Aimee. 'Talk is they're gonna hang him as soon as the sheriff gets back.'

'Surely there'll be a trial afore they can hang anybody. At least that's how it's done in most places.'

The storekeeper arrived with the coffee and overheard Cyriac.

'Huh,' he snorted, 'this is Thomaston. The law here don't bother with courts and judges. They just hang anyone as crosses them.'

Cyriac sipped thoughtfully at his coffee. 'Mighty fine coffee you serve up.'

The storekeeper, a rangy man with angular jaw and huge moustache, straightened his shoulders.

'My wife makes it,' he said, a note of pride in his voice. 'Won't let no one else mess with it. She got her own special way of doing it and it sure works good. She's a fine cook, too. If you want to sample her cooking tonight you'll have to get in early as the place fills up quick.'

Cyriac frowned and stared into his coffee before answering.

'No, I got an invite to supper already. Maybe some other time.'

'You don't know what you're missing, mister.'

The storekeeper went back to his duties, leaving Cyriac and the women to discuss the latest developments.

'What are we going to do, Mr Halkias?' Beth asked. 'We can't let them hang the poor man.'

Cyriac lifted the cup and drank.

'First off, begin by calling me Cyriac. I never did cotton to this mister business. You say they got him in jail. Ain't much we can do about that.'

Beth's small hand reached out and placed it on Cyriac's.

'Please.'

69

Cyriac gazed down at that hand on his big paw, no heavier than a butterfly, and he wondered if Lily Benedict's hand had looked like that before she was murdered. At the same time, the image of Arlene McCullough surfaced and the brutal hands of the lawman pawing her.

'It ain't none of my business,' he said without much conviction.

'Let the mangy hound hang,' Aimee said. 'He'll be no loss to nobody.'

'Aimee, how can you say such a thing? I sometimes despair of you. He never did us no harm and he even agreed to let us share his cabin.'

Cyriac looked from one woman to the other and not for the first time wondered if they really were sisters; Beth so fine and gentle and Aimee harsh and unforgiving. And then he remembered Beth saying they were half-sisters and with that came the memory of his own brother.

Was that how folks saw him – the insensitive brute – the reverse of his sibling? What would Milo have done? He had asked Cyriac to look after Turlough. He placed his free hand on top of Beth's – resting so lightly on his.

'You like Turlough?' he asked.

Beth flushed and looked down at his hand on hers.

'It's just that he's so young – no more than a boy,' she whispered. 'Nobody deserves to be hung without a fair trial. It just ain't right.'

Cyriac recovered his hand and getting up, walked across to the storekeeper.

'The fella as was with these young ladies and was arrested is a friend of mine. I need a lawyer to defend him. I wonder if you could direct me as to where I can find one.'

The man fingered his luxuriant moustache as he spoke.

'Temba is your nearest bet. But you would be wasting your time and money. I just told you there won't be a trial.

Your friend will be taken out some morning and hanged.'

'Where can I find this Sheriff Ginsberg then? Perhaps I can appeal to him.'

'Mister, have you ever tried parleying with a grizzly? Cos you'd have more chance with the bear as getting anywhere with the sheriff.'

'I don't suppose you would join us for coffee? I'd like to get the lowdown on how things work around here.'

'Sure thing, mister. I'll get Martha to make a fresh pot and then I'll be with you.'

Cyriac introduced Beth and Aimee to the storekeeper when he arrived with the coffee.

'If the store gets busy I'll have to leave you. My name is Stan Richards. Elwood Black is a businessman as runs things around here. Sheriff Ginsberg is his man. You have to pay them a tax so as to stay in business. Anyone as refuses to pay doesn't last. Ginsberg sets his deputies on them and they end up in jail or get beat up. They prey on the miners as well. Harassing and bullying them into giving up their claims. Only I got so much sunk in this store I'd move on elsewhere.' He shook his head in frustration. 'I keep thinking things gotta get better.'

'Do you know where the sheriff is now?'

'Yeah, he and Black run fighting bouts. Ginsberg is their star fighter. The Fighting Sheriff they call him. They put up big prize money so as to tempt anyone to challenge him. He's never lost a fight yet. Ginsberg has killed a few in the ring. He's unbeatable. He and Black went out some days ago to organize a fight in Rivesville. I guess he's due back any time soon.'

'The Fighting Sheriff,' Cyriac repeated, shaking his head bemusedly. 'Helluva way to make a living.'

'Oh, he enjoys it. I saw him fight. They had a few bouts here in Thomaston and the money was too tempting for some. Now folk around here know better than to challenge him. That's why Ginsberg has to go further and further afield to get fights. Some place as folk mightn't have heard of him.'

'So what do you reckon will happen to our friend Benedict?'

'They'll hang him for sure. His pa struck lucky. He came into town with a sack full of nuggets. Then he got in a poker game and had an argument with the gunman, Clive Carter, who accused him of cheating. Next thing Benedict is dead. The samples of gold he brought in with him disappeared at the same time. Then Turlough has a fight with Carter's sidekick, Alfie Manning. Sometime later Manning is found dead. Turlough swears he didn't kill him. You can put your own slant on things. A man makes a big strike and one by one his family is killed or driven away. With no one to work the claim, Alliance Holdings, which is owned by Black, will take it over.'

'How terrible,' exclaimed Beth, 'can nothing be done to right this?'

Richards glanced around the store, suddenly nervous.

'Maybe I said too much. You never heard any of this from me. I'd better get back to work.'

'It seems pretty hopeless,' Beth said when the storekeeper left. 'It looks like they'll hang Turlough and take over his family's claim. There's nothing anyone can do about it.'

People were coming and going in the store while the three sat there; each of them sunk in their own dire thoughts. They looked up as Richards came over.

'I just heard, the sheriff is back in town.'

'Thanks,' Cyriac said. 'Maybe I should just mosey down there and have a talk with him.'

The storekeeper shook his head. 'Remember what I said about having a parley with a grizzly. You'll be wasting your time.'

72

Cyriac stood up. 'Nevertheless I'd like to try.'

Beth stood, too. 'I'll go with you.'

'You'd better not get involved,' Cyriac advised.

'I am involved,' Beth said. She turned to the store-keeper. 'Mr Richards, can you make a pot of coffee and make up some vittles? Poor Turlough must be pretty hungry by now.'

# 16

Cyriac stepped inside the sheriff's office, followed by the two women. Aimee had decided to come too and he wondered if it was only to mock the prisoner. Inside was a man about Cyriac's own age in a broadcloth suit with collar and necktie. He was seated with a heavily built man wearing a sheriff's badge on his vest. The sheriff had a brutal face and was hatless, exposing a bald head. The two men were in earnest discussion but looked up when Cyriac entered.

'Yeah?' the sheriff said with no hint of friendliness in his voice.

'I believe you got a prisoner in here – name of Turlough Benedict.'

'What's it to you?'

'We brought some grub for him,' Cyriac said, indicating the basket Beth was carrying.

'Leave it. I'll see he gets it.'

Jesse Linenan chose that moment to come out from the cells, rubbing his knuckles.

'I just gave that punk a good working over,' he said

before his jaw dropped and he slapped his hand on his gun. 'That's the son of a bitch as buffaloed me!' he yelled, then stopped as he saw the gun in Cyriac's hand.

'Howdy, Jesse. I came back to return the gun you loaned me. You can have it back, either barrel first or butt first.'

'What the hell's going on?' the sheriff roared. 'Put that gun away, fella, afore I arrest you.'

'I don't mind putting the gun down as long as you can control your deputy here.'

There was a sudden movement as the sheriff abruptly stood, toppling the chair he was sitting on. He was a giant of a man, reaching well over six and a half feet, and broad and muscular.

'Mister, you're obviously a stranger round here. I'm Sheriff Ginsberg. You don't put that gun up, I'll shoot you down for disobeying a law officer.'

'As a legitimate citizen of the United States of America, I have every right to carry a gun and defend myself. I just heard your deputy here boasting of giving your prisoner a good going over. That don't seem very law-abiding behaviour. In view of my suspicions, I claim the right to hold this gun until I am sure I am in no danger from no trigger happy *hombres*, even if they are acting under the cloak of lawmen. I've seen your brand of law and it ain't like no law I am familiar with.'

The atmosphere in the office was tense as Cyriac casually held Linenan's gun, waiting for the sheriff and his deputy to make their play. It was plain Ginsberg was itching to pull his gun and have it out with the stranger. But then, Cyriac had the advantage with a gun already in his hand. It could go either way. Men would die and the lawmen were wondering which of them the stranger would shoot first before the other got a shot off.

'Whoa there.' The man in the suit stood up, holding his

hands out wide from his sides. 'This ain't no way to settle an argument. Sit down, Goren.' He flapped a hand at Ginsberg and surprisingly the lawman sat. 'Jesse, you sit, too.'

Sullenly the deputy came across and perched on the edge of the sheriff's desk.

'Mister, I didn't catch your name. You can put that gun up and we'll talk this over peaceable.'

'Halkias is the name.' Cyriac did not surrender his gun but lowered it by his side. 'You have a friend of mine in your cells and I came by here to find out how he's faring, only to discover a pair of bullyboy lawmen beating up on helpless prisoners. Under the circumstances I don't rate his chances of survival very high.'

'My name is Elwood Black and I'm not without influence about these parts. What is the name of this prisoner you are enquiring about?'

'Turlough Benedict.'

'What exactly is your relationship with Mr Benedict? Are you a relation?'

Remembering the storekeeper telling of how anyone with a worthwhile mining claim was killed or driven off, Cyriac decided to play a bluff.

'We're partners in a mining claim. I bought into a half share with him.'

The frown was fleeting but Cyriac was watching for a reaction.

'I see, and have you any proof of such a transaction?'

'Yep, the papers are lodged with my lawyer in Temba,' Cyriac lied smoothly, then stopped abruptly and frowned as if he had a sudden thought. 'There was a clause that if either of us died the other's half of the claim would pass to the surviving partner.'

He stood staring off into the distance as if the significance of this had just occurred to him. The mine owner was also frowning as he thought over what the other man had revealed.

'So if your friend was to be found guilty of murder and hanged, it would not be a worry to you?'

Cyriac snapped back into focus again. 'Of course it would. I don't want no harm coming to him.'

Black was staring speculatively at Cyriac. 'Are you a betting man, Mr Halkias?'

'What's that got to do with anything?'

'Sheriff Ginsberg and I run a little sideline. We organize boxing bouts. You look as if you've been in a fight or two. How about I propose a little wager? You take on my man in the ring and if you win, your friend Benedict goes free.'

'That's no kinda bet. I'll hire a lawyer and fight the case in court. Your wager doesn't take into account Benedict's guilt or innocence. That wouldn't tempt me to get in no ring with no bruiser. What if I lose? I'm no better off except a few new scars to add to these.' Cyriac pointed to his heavily marked face. 'No deal, mister.'

'Wait, I can make it worth your while. What if I put up a purse of five thousand dollars?'

Cyriac laughed harshly. 'That claim is worth much more than that. We could dig five thousand dollars out in less than a month.'

This last assertion was only a guess but he could see from Black's face it had hit home.

'Ten thousand then against your half of the claim.'

Cyriac stared speculatively at the mine owner. 'Ten thousand, you say?' Slowly he nodded. 'That might be worth fighting for. I'd want to see the money up front.'

Black bridled at this. 'You saying you don't trust my word?'

'Mister, I just met you. You seem to hang around with some unsavoury people. They say you can tell a man by the company he keeps. So no, I don't trust you. We'll need a

76

neutral body to hold the stakes.'

'All right then, who do you suggest?'

'Doc McCullough seems to be an honourable man. You give him a promissory note for $10,000 and I'll sign a paper deeding my half of the claim to you on the occasion that I lose the fight. Who have you in mind that I take on?'

Elwood Black was grinning broadly as he turned and pointed to the sheriff.

'There's my man.'

Cyriac took a step backward, his face creasing in a worried frown. 'You mean I gotta fight the sheriff?'

Relishing Cyriac's feigned discomfort, Black waved a hand in the direction of the cells.

'Now we have agreed the terms of your partner's release, you can take him his lunch.'

Cyriac nodded to Beth and they walked forward. As they came near the desk Linenan gave them a venomous look.

'What about my gun?' he snarled.

Cyriac tossed the weapon at the deputy. He fumbled but caught it before it fell to the floor. Linenan was frowning at the gun in his hand.

'Son of a bitch,' he muttered. 'It ain't loaded.'

# 17

Cyriac stood on the porch, hat in hand and stared stoically at the door knocker.

'Hell,' he muttered and turned to leave.

The door opened and Arlene McCullough stood there

smiling at him and a strange shivery feeling guttered through Cyriac, leaving him feeling helpless as well as speechless.

'Cyriac, how lovely. I didn't hear you knock.'

He stood big and awkwardly on the stoop, dumb as a pole-axed buffalo. Arlene stepped back.

'Come on in. It was getting late and I wondered if you'd forgotten.'

'No, ma'am, I mean, miss, I'd not forgot.'

He was inside the hall and there was no going back.

'Let me take your hat.'

She eased it from his grip and smiled at him. The hallway seemed to brighten with that smile. Cyriac blinked and tried a smile in return that didn't quite make it all the way. He swallowed.

'Thank you, miss.'

'Arlene, please call me Arlene.'

The doctor appeared in the hallway. 'Is that our guest? Come on in, Mr Halkias. Would a little snorter be in order before supper?'

Cyriac shambled down the hall, feeling clumsy as a carthorse.

'Don't drink too much, you two,' Arlene called. 'Supper is almost ready.'

The doctor poured whiskeys for them. While they waited, someone knocked on the door.

'Damn it, this always happens,' the doctor grumbled. 'Just as I am about to sit down to a meal or a quiet drink, someone comes needing my services.'

The two men sipped their drinks and listened to the murmur of voices. Arlene must have resolved the matter for there was no call for the doctor and shortly she summoned them to eat. A manila envelope was propped on the sideboard with Doctor McCullough's name printed across it.

'What's this?'

'It's just been delivered.'

Cyriac was staring nervously at the table loaded down with silverware and food. Hell, when was the last time he had sat at a table as elegant as this?

The golden brown carcass of a chicken steamed slightly in the centre while tureens gave off tantalizing aromas. The doctor had opened the envelope and was reading.

'What the hell. . . ?'

'Language, Pa, at the dining table,' Arlene chided.

McCullough was holding the paper and staring across at Cyriac.

'This is a promissory note to pay you the sum of $10,000 in the event of your beating Goren Ginsberg in a pugilistic match to be staged the day after tomorrow. Fourteenth of April 1888.'

Arlene was gaping at Cyriac, a shocked look on her face. 'You can't do this,' she gasped.

Cyriac was looking down at his plate, so white against the pristine whiteness of the table linen, and his own hands so gnarled and discoloured and out of place in this refined dining room.

'I gotta go,' he said and stood.

He did not get to the door before Arlene was there before him, holding on to his arm, feeling she was gripping a timber truss, hard and unyielding.

'I'm sorry. Do please sit down again.'

He looked into her eyes and all his resolve melted before that earnest gaze. He felt weak as a newborn calf. Meekly he allowed her to guide him back to the chair.

'Father, sit down. No more talk about wagers or fighting. We are going to sit and enjoy this supper that I went to such trouble to prepare.'

79

They ate the meal with Arlene and her pa making small talk about local events and people they knew. From time to time Arlene tried to draw Cyriac but he contributed very little. He was content to sit there in that special place listening to them and thinking how civilized it was.

He recalled an incident when he had been holed up, waiting for the men who had been sent to kill him and while he watched, a brightly painted bunting had landed close to his hiding place.

The bird began to sing and nearby another answered. Undetected by the birds and cradling his killing implements, he had been immensely saddened as he listened to the birds singing. So moved had he been that he had resolved to creep away from that place of death. But before he could do so, the birds had been disturbed as the killers moved in. The exotic bunting had fluttered away, taking with it all feelings of goodwill and mercy.

Arlene and her father were like that bird and its mate with their refrain of warmth and amity. Being here with them induced in him a rare feeling of harmony and a delicious quickening of his blood. Mixed with these feelings, he also felt an intense sadness, for he knew this place and these people were immeasurably separate from him. He ate his meal, clearing all that was served up to him, savouring the excellent food and favouring that interlude as if it were to be his last evening on earth.

When the meal was finished, he was invited to join them in the parlour. He was almost inclined to refuse and leave but knew it would be pure churlishness on his part.

'Brandy?' Arlene queried when they were seated.

While Arlene served up the drinks, Doctor McCullough offered him a fat cigar and they lit up. The civilized behaviour of his hosts served to heighten Cyriac's isolation.

'I used to spar a bit when I was younger,' the doctor

offered. 'Maybe I can give you a few pointers.'

'I would appreciate that,' Cyriac said, thinking the doctor's concept of fighting would be completely irrelevant to the tactics that would be employed in his coming bout with Sheriff Ginsberg.

The only rule was that there would be no rules. The contestants would try to put each other in the dirt by whatever means possible. And the man to go down would be the man destined never to get up again.

Arlene was mostly silent during this exchange, taking small sips of her drink. Cyriac was acutely aware of her scrutiny and it made him deeply self-conscious. However, he was determined to allow himself this rare oasis of peace and serenity.

'I was told you came into town in the company of two women,' Arlene said at one stage. 'Are they friends of yours?'

'I only just met them. When I came into Gold Point with Benedict they had taken over his empty cabin. They were kind enough to accompany him into town to enquire about his mother who seems to have disappeared.'

'An unfortunate family,' the doctor contributed. 'I hear they slung the youngster in jail. Knowing Ginsberg, they'll in all likelihood hang him.'

'I guess that's how the law in these parts operate,' Cyriac averred. 'Do you know anything of this Carter gang that runs with Black?'

'I know enough to advise anyone to steer clear of them. A gang of killers and bandits. Black employs them from time to time as enforcers. But he has to be careful. Let those hellhounds loose on a town and come nightfall, there would be nothing left of it.'

'I see. Where do they hang out?'

'Black houses them out at his mine. He uses them as

bodyguards and heaven knows what else. I'd as soon keep a nest of rattlers in my surgery as give room to that bunch of killers. Every one of that gang is ornery as a polecat with a thorn in its paw and liable to shoot you for just looking at them.'

The evening grew late and Cyriac knew he had to depart. Reluctantly he rose to take his leave, knowing this would be his last taste of genteel society. Arlene accompanied him to the front door.

'Thank you for the delightful meal,' he said.

'Why are you doing this, Cyriac?'

'Why, it's getting late and I can't impose any more on you and your pa,' he said, even though he knew quite well she did not have in mind his departure.

'I mean this fight with Ginsberg. I've heard terrible things about him. He has killed men in these bouts. The man is an animal. Ride away, Cyriac. No one will think any the less of you.'

He turned to look up into the sky, seeing the canopy of the night studded with clusters of sparkling diamonds, then he turned back and saw the twin jewels of tears in her eyes. Her hand came up and her fingers briefly touched his lips with the soft touch of a moth and like that delicate insect, she was noiselessly gone, the door closing softly behind her.

# 18

Thomaston was buzzing. The saloons were doing a roaring trade. Horses, carts and wagons lined the roads and side streets as people came in from the outlaying areas and townships to witness the fight. Elwood Black had sent riders out with printed posters as soon as he knew he had snared Cyriac.

The event was to be a big affair. An army of labourers from Black's mining operations were recruited to erect a giant marquee on the outskirts of the town. As the crowds swirled around the stores and the saloons, children ran wild, excited by the hurly-burly going on around them.

The bout was scheduled to take place at three o'clock in the afternoon when the light was good and people wouldn't be too drunk to attend. The same labourers who erected the tent would be retained to keep order.

Already the betting was heating up. The odds against Cyriac were at one hundred to one. The odds shortened when betting on how long he would last. Going one round was ten to one with the odds lengthening with each subsequent round.

Cyriac had ridden back to the Benedict shack with the sisters. He spent the spare time patching up the place; replacing boards, and fixing broken windows and steps. The materials for these jobs he was able to scrounge or buy from the neighbouring miners working the diggings.

Once they knew who he was, they were more than willing to help and some even offered to assist with the repairs. These offers Cyriac declined. He needed to be on his own or at least to work alone while he awaited his rendezvous with Sheriff Ginsberg.

Watching him work, no one would have guessed he had a date with the deadliest pugilist ever to fight in those parts. Such was the sheriff's reputation that Elwood Black had been forced to go further and further afield to find fighters willing to go against his champion. Tricking Cyriac had been an inspiration and one Black knew would pay off.

Not only would the mine owner be rid of a troublemaker, he would be another step closer to getting his hands on the Benedict mining claim.

Cyriac worked steadily, stopping only for drinks and the meals that Beth provided. On the morning of the fight, he ate a large breakfast of eggs, fatback and freshly baked bread washed down with lashings of coffee.

'I don't know how you can scoff all that, knowing what is going to happen today,' Beth said. 'I couldn't eat a thing.'

'This is all I will eat today until the fight is over,' Cyriac told her.

'Aren't you worried?'

'What good would that do?'

'If you hadn't got involved with that dimwit Benedict,' Aimee told him sourly, 'you wouldn't be in this bother. Why you care about that loser beats me. If it were me I would just ride away.'

'I guess,' was Cyriac's only response.

He went outside and continued his work. From time to time miners came by to chat but Cyriac's dogged silence discouraged them and they left him alone, watching him from a distance.

In the afternoon a buckboard came bouncing along the bottom of the valley and pulled up nearby. Cyriac glanced idly at the occupant and straightened up from his task when he recognized him.

'Howdy, Cyriac,' Doc McCullough called. 'I've come to give you a ride into town.'

'What makes you think I'm going in?'

'You're not the sort of man who walks away.'

'I'll manage OK on my own.'

'Yeah, I know you will but I thought you might like one friend by your side. I'm volunteering to be your second.'

Cyriac was shaking his head. 'I can't let you do that, Doc. It'll be too dangerous.'

'Hah!' the doctor barked out a laugh. 'I was a surgeon in the war when this country was tearing itself apart. I've been through more hell and brimstone than you could ever imagine. Don't talk to me about danger. Now go and fetch your coat and get in this damn cart afore I change my mind.'

Cyriac studied the doctor for a few moments before turning indoors and remerging with his coat and his gun belt.

'You won't be able to wear that during the fight,' McCullough said. 'It is fisticuffs, not a gun duel.'

'I won't be wearing it but you will. If you are determined to be my second then you need to keep this handy in case I need it.'

'Thomaston is thick with people,' Doc McCullough said. 'Black is a snake but even he won't dare try anything underhand with such a crowd in town. You'll be safe enough for today at least. Well, as safe as anyone going into the ring with that gorilla Ginsberg.'

They were some miles down the road before Cyriac spoke again.

'Did she send you?'

'Can't you say her name then?' the doctor asked testily. 'She! What way is that to refer to someone whose life you've turned upside down? Call her by her God given name if you want to talk about her.'

'What?'

'Ask me again, but this time ask properly.'

'What do you mean I turned her life upside down?' Cyriac muttered.

'You blind, dumb, big ox.' The doctor sighed heavily. 'Arlene is the most precious thing in my life. I've watched

85

over her since her fiancée died last year.'

'How did he die?'

'It was an accident up at Black's mining operation. God help me but I could not bring myself to tell Arlene, but my suspicions were that it was no accident. Robert was a surveyor and assayer. My guess was he found something dodgy at Alliance Holdings and was killed to keep him quiet.'

They drove in silence for a while, Cyriac mulling over what the doctor had just told him. It was only when the town came into sight that the doctor spoke again.

'I ain't ever seen the town so lively. It seems the whole country has come to see you fight. There's still time to reconsider.'

'Doc, I thought you came to be my second, not try and talk me down.'

McCullough grinned at him. 'Afore I left town this morning I bet on the outcome of the fight. I got good odds, too: one hundred to one. I wagered twenty dollars.'

Beth watched the buggy driving away with Cyriac and the doctor.

'Come on, sis, we gotta go in and give Cyriac some support.'

'Huh!' Aimee snorted but went willingly to saddle up.

When the women got to town, there were so many pedestrians milling about and vehicles parked everywhere and anywhere that they were at a loss as to where to look for Cyriac.

Beth said, 'Seeing it was the doctor that took him in his buggy that's where he'll be at.'

After making enquiries they were directed to the doctor's surgery. Arlene opened the door to them.

'I'm afraid the doctor is not in. He went off some time ago and I don't know when to expect him back again.'

'Oh dear. The doctor is with a friend of ours and we were hoping to join them.' Beth turned to go. 'Thank you, miss.'

Arlene was frowning. 'A friend, you say. Who might that be?'

'Mr Halkias; Doctor McCullough drove off with him in his buggy.'

Arlene's frown deepened. She stepped back from the door.

'Please come in.'

The girls filed into the parlour.

'Now tell me exactly what my father is doing with Mr Halkias.'

## 19

The noise in and around the giant marquee was akin to that of a hungry beast as the area seethed with men hungry to watch the fight – billed as the greatest match of the nineteenth century. The challenger, Goren Ginsberg, was being promoted as the man to defeat the famous John L. Sullivan, only for the fact the champion was afraid to face Thomaston's sheriff. Halkias became the Greek Gorilla from the land of ancient heroes.

Elwood Black, fat cigar jammed between his teeth, strolled through the packed crowds, his passage eased by the wedge of bullyboys roughly forcing their way through the yelling, howling mob of eager fight fans. He pushed inside one of the makeshift pens erected to house the combatants and give them some privacy from the eager fans.

Sheriff Ginsberg was sitting on a stool naked except for a pair of long drawers. His body was being liberally smeared with grease while his arms and legs were vigorously massaged by a quartet of helpers. The two men nodded and grinned at each other.

'Don't finish this too quickly, Goren,' Black said. 'The punters will want their money's worth. Give them three, maybe four or five rounds.'

The giant fighter swilled from a water jug, gargling it in his mouth before spitting into a bucket. He then picked up a whiskey bottle and took a slug from that.

'What if he falls down with fright?' Ginsberg grunted. 'Hell, he might pass out after I hit him.'

'Don't be too cocky with this one. There's something about this fella strikes me as his being a tough hombre. He thought nothing of facing us down in the jail singlehanded – and with an empty pistol. The way Masterson tells it, he faced down Jesse Linenan at the doc's place and put them both to flight. We want this Cyriac Halkias dead all right, but do it right and make sure when he goes down he stays down.'

'Since when did I ever fail you, boss?' Ginsberg lifted a huge hand and formed it into a fist. It looked as big and hard as one of the buffalo skulls that littered the prairie. 'Just watch these fists punch that greaser into an early grave. No one can stand against these hammers of death.'

'Good.' Black slapped Ginsberg on the shoulder and then took a towel to wipe the grease from his hand. 'I'll go and have a word with our referee, Jemmy Walbeck. He knows the score and will be on your side all the way.'

'I tell you,' Ginsburg growled, 'I don't need no one on my side. Only one man will walk outta that ring today and that'll be yours truly.'

'Nevertheless I like to figure all the angles.'

A few strides away in another cubical, the challenger was also sitting on a stool and Doctor McCullough was with him. He was instructing Cyriac on the art of fisticuffs. His pupil was sitting with closed eyes and McCullough was not sure if his pupil was listening. The doctor was distracted by the number of scars and the puckered marks of old wounds that had been stitched together without much skill, giving a rough and uneven texture to Cyriac's torso.

'You don't mix with this gorilla. He's as strong as a bull and if he gets inside, he's liable to pound your guts to mincemeat. Dance around hitting him but keeping out of range. Hell, damn it, are you even listening to me?'

Cyriac opened his eyes nodded and reached for the water jug. The doctor slapped his hand away.

'Don't take anything that is supplied by that snake Black. You can't tell what it's laced with.' The doctor reached in his bag and handed Cyriac a flask. 'I brought our own refreshments.'

Cyriac drank while the doctor continued coaching him.

'Grease,' Cyriac interrupted him. 'I need to grease my body.'

'Yeah, I got the grease.'

Again the doctor reached in his bag and brought out a large tub and unscrewed the top. He dipped in and produced a generous blob of yellowish cream. Cyriac wrinkled his nose as his friend slapped the mixture on his chest and began to smear it in.

'What the hell is that? It smells like something crawled in that jar and died.'

'This is good stuff,' the doctor said, dipping in for more grease. 'It's my own concoction; a mixture of lard, alcohol and urine.'

'Sweet mother of all my woes! Why couldn't you just have made do with axle grease?'

89

'The lard is made from beef fat. If you get weary during the fight just lick your arms. The fat will nourish you while the alcohol will fire up your flagging spirits.'

Cyriac raised his eyebrows.

'A joke,' the doc said and put more of the mixture on. 'And before you ask, the urine is a healing agent. Trust me. I have been preparing for this fight since you told me about it, so try and be grateful. Like I say, I don't trust anything supplied by Elwood Black. Also, I have a stake in you winning.

'I went into Ginsberg's booth a while back and asked to inspect what they were using on their fighter. On the pretext of examining the water I slipped in a sleeping draught. So watch for him yawning. That's when you move in and put him to sleep permanent like.'

A slow and rare smile broke across Cyriac's uneven features.

'McCullough, remind me to change my doctor after this. You're as cunning as a sack of raccoons. A fella wouldn't know what the hell you'd be slipping him on the pretext of curing him.'


'So Cyriac was tricked into this fight just because he was trying to save his friend, Turlough?' Arlene asked.

Beth nodded. 'That awful sheriff told Cyriac he would hang Turlough and then offered him a chance to save him if he fought him in a boxing match. Cyriac and Benedict are partners in a mining claim. If Cyriac loses then his share of the mine will be given over to Black, but whatever happens, he promised Turlough would go free. Cyriac had no choice – if he wanted to save Turlough he had to fight.'

'Dear God,' Arlene said in a low, trembling voice. 'Ginsberg has killed men in the ring and out of the ring if the truth be told. He wants Cyriac dead otherwise he wouldn't have challenged him. They covet the Benedict claim. Whichever way things go they will kill Cyriac and Turlough will be dead soon after. They murdered his sister and now his mother is missing. I think the Benedict claim is so rich Black is prepared to go to any lengths to take it over. It's what they do.

'Poor Cyriac is caught up in this terrible mess. He will not live out this day. And my father is with him. I fear for him, too.' She got up from her chair and paced up and down. 'Dear God, what can we do?' She sat down again, staring at her guests with stricken eyes. 'I feel so helpless. If only we could help in some way.'

Aimee stood up. 'I'll go down and see what I can find out.'

Arlene was shaking her head. 'Women aren't allowed in the arena. They'll never let you in.' She looked at the big woman with her angular shape and sharp features. 'Wait a moment. You might just pass as . . . wait a minute . . . there is a spare medical bag.'

Arlene left the room, leaving the sisters wondering what she was up to.

## 20

The crowd roared as the fat man clambered into the ring. Jemmy Walbeck was an imposing figure in a suit straining at the seams to contain his corpulent figure.

'Gentlemen and ladies,' he bellowed. Like everything

about him, Walbeck's voice was also big. The noise from the crowd lessened. 'Oh, I forgot, no ladies are present.' Walbeck guffawed at his own joke.

'Give over, you pudding belly buffoon,' someone shouted. 'Get on with the fight.'

'Come on, you baldpate scoundrel,' another called, referring to Walbeck's glistening scalp, 'we didn't pay to hear your greasy ranting.'

But Walbeck could give as good as he got.

'Who let this clay-brained loon in? I believe you must have slept in the cesspit last night. I can smell you from here.'

The banter went on for some time – the compère rousing the crowd with jokes and lewd remarks. The horde of onlookers loved it and at times the arena rocked with shouts of laughter. At last Walbeck brought the teasing to an end and began the build up to the fight.

'You have here today the greatest fighter the world has ever seen. The unbeatable, the unparalleled, the giant of the fighting game. The winner of numerous bouts and, to crown it all, the best lawman in the whole of the west. I give you Sheriff Goren Ginsberg.'

The champion strode out of his cubical, looking bigger than ever with great slabs of muscle on his chest and arms and shoulders. The roar from the crowd had something bestial about it. He ducked through the ropes and to the great delight of the crowd, began shadow boxing. The compère had trouble calming the crowd sufficiently to introduce the contender.

'Against this giant of strength and fighting skill comes an indubitable challenger. May I introduce Kratos the Greek god from the other side of the world.' Walbeck was allowing his imagination full rein. 'He has won so many bouts in Europe that he has run out of opponents. Now he has travelled to our own United States of America to fight our champion, Sheriff Ginsberg.'

It was Cyriac's turn to step out and make his way to the ring. Dark and muscled, he carried more scars than his opponent. He slipped into the ring and stood quietly in one corner. Cyriac was a big man but he looked diminished beside the sheer bulk of Ginsberg. The crowd grew quiet as they took in the disparity between the fighters; the huge bulk of Ginsberg and the more compact, muscular form of Cyriac.

Doctor McCullough followed, carrying his medicine bag and settled down in Cyriac's corner. The referee beckoned the fighters to the centre of the ring. The contrast in size was even more striking as the two men moved up face to face.

'I'm gonna eat your heart, little man,' Ginsberg sneered. 'Any last requests? Maybe you wanna be buried alongside your murdering partner Benedict. Sure as the sun comes up tomorrow morning, I'm gonna hang him.'

'I was told he would go free, no matter the outcome of this bout,' Cyriac said.

'Elwood Black made that promise to you, but I ain't beholden to any undertaking Black makes.' Ginsberg jabbed himself in the chest with a thick thumb. 'I am the law. I make the law. I carry out the law. The law demands a death for a death.'

Cyriac stared steadily back at the sheriff. 'So be it,' he said slowly, 'a death for a death.'

'Back to your corners,' Walbeck roared and the crowd roared with him.

The fight was on.

With a big smirk on his face, the sheriff of Thomaston strode across the ring and swung a haymaker at his opponent that had it landed, it would most likely have batted

Cyriac out of the ring. Cyriac ducked beneath it and punched two hard jabs into Ginsberg's kidneys. With a roar of rage, Ginsberg turned and came again at the smaller man. Cyriac danced out of range but not before he put another couple of jabs into the other fighter's belly.

Cyriac was moving easily and smoothly on his feet, dancing out of range as his bigger opponent tried to close in on him. When the bell went Ginsberg had not landed a punch on Cyriac. The big man was scowling as he stood in his corner, glugging from a bottle and spitting out into a bucket.

'This sleeping potion of yours doesn't seem to be working,' Cyriac muttered to McCullough as the doctor pumped his arms and rubbed more fat on his face.

'Goddamn it, he's spitting the water in a bucket. How was I to know? You're doing well. Just keep out of his reach. I've seen him fight. If he gets you in a bear hug he'll finish you.'

The bell sounded for the second round and the fighters came out of their corners. Again Ginsberg tried rushing Cyriac but the other man was expecting him and danced out of range again, driving those deadly punches into the kidneys. This time Ginsberg winced when they landed, for Cyriac had punched him time and time again in the same place. Rounds two and three were repeats of the first with Cyriac untouched while peppering his bigger opponent with rapid fire punches either to the kidneys or the abdomen.

Ginsberg roared like a wounded bear, growling at Cyriac. Telling him to stand and fight like a man. But Cyriac had adopted a workmanlike approach to the fight. He danced around, keeping well out of reach of those mallet-like fists that looked as though they would give one solidly landed blow to finish him.

94

'He's beginning to get winded,' the doctor told Cyriac in between rounds. 'But it'll take more than that to finish him.

Cyriac was looking past his second and could see Elwood Black in conference with the referee, who was leaning out over the ropes to listen to the mine owner. He wondered what was being cooked up. Warily he came out of his corner. Ginsberg had given up rushing at him but began stalking him instead.

'Come to me, little man,' he coaxed. 'I have something here that will loosen your head from your shoulders.' And he brandished his huge ham-like fists at Cyriac.

His opponent did not respond to the invitation other than dance out of range and then manoeuvre temptingly close, which had the big man swinging wildly, leaving himself open to another tattoo of punches from the smaller, swifter moving man.

As Cyriac skipped away from Ginsberg, he crashed into something solid, taking him completely by surprise. A hard shove from behind and he realized he had blundered into the referee. But he had no time to wonder how that had happened, for with a triumphant grin, Ginsberg came at him swinging. This time Cyriac had no room to dodge.

Something with the weight and texture of a side of beef hit him in the face and he cannoned back, trying desperately to backpedal but again he crashed into the referee and was bounced back within range of those brutal fists. A hammer blow to his chest sent him to his knees and then a pile driver on the top of his head and his senses were spinning. Another fist hit him on the temple and he went over backwards. He saw the boot coming and tried to roll with it. Something with the consistency of a fence post whacked into the back of his head and blackness enveloped him, blocking out the agonizing pain.

**21**

Someone had stuffed a dead skunk into his nose and as he breathed, the pungent odour convulsed his lungs and he coughed. He tried not to breathe but the pain in his head made him gasp and again that overpowering smell seized his lungs. It was as if he was drowning. He coughed and fought against the cloying smell and intense pain that was pulling him down.

Cyriac opened his eyes and saw the anxious face of Doctor McCullough. The doctor was pushing a cloth in his face and it was this that was suffocating him.

'Damn you,' he muttered and pushed the doctor away.

The smell lessened somewhat but it was still there, biting into his nostrils and he shook his head and shards of metal gouged the inside of his skull. He stopped moving.

'Cyriac, I'm stopping the fight.'

'The hell you say?'

Cyriac was replaying the sequence of events; the referee conferring with Black and his subsequent interfering in the fight. It was all coming back. And with it, that familiar coldness; starting somewhere in the base of his skull and slowly spreading.

'No,' he whispered but it was to no avail – the deadly resolve was taking over – blotting out the pain. His vision took on a crimson tinge – he could not help the smile that spread itself across his face.

Doctor McCullough was bending down, peering into his

96

face and saying something but Cyriac ignored him. Another shape loomed behind the doctor. It was Jemmy Walbeck, the referee, frowning and shaking his head, looking down at Cyriac, trying to look sympathetic and failing, a malicious glint in his eyes as he gazed at the stricken fighter.

'You want to call it off, Doc? Your man looks in a bad way.'

'You fat, greasy lout,' the doctor snarled. 'You interfered with my fighter. You're not fit to be a referee. You should be cleaning out spittoons instead of officiating at a fight. If you ever come in my surgery needing treatment it'll put you to sleep permanently.'

'Now, now, Doc, that's not very professional. Your man was so busy running away he accidentally bumped into me. I could have been badly injured. I might sue for damages.'

Cyriac stood. He was still smiling and all the while looking at Walbeck. The punch did not travel far. It sank into the large man's belly and he bent over with an audible whoosh of breath. As the referee folded over, Cyriac head butted that fat face and Walbeck flopped on the deck like a stranded whale, blood spurting from his busted nose.

Cyriac stepped over the collapsed man and walked across the ring, everything slowing down around him. The noise of the crowd became muted.

Ginsberg was grinning and gesturing to the crowd. The roar went up a notch or two when they saw Cyriac emerge from his corner. Ginsberg looked at Cyriac and his grin grew wider. The champion waved to the crowd and stepped towards his rival. Cyriac came straight at him, ducking under a vicious hook from his opponent. Once more he punched into the sheriff's belly.

Ginsberg was built like a sodbuster's shack with layers of muscle protecting him. Cyriac felt the shock run up his

97

arm as his fist drove into the sheriff's abdomen, solid as a door. Ginsberg grunted and stepped back, visibly shaken. Cyriac smiled up at him and punched with the other fist. Again the sheriff went backwards and at the same time swung at his opponent. Cyriac dropped to one knee and the big fist sailed over the top of his head.

Again he punched Ginsberg's midriff, this time the blow driving upwards and crunching into the rib cage. Ginsberg opened his mouth and gasped in agony as something bust in his chest. He leaned forward, his mouth gaping open as he tried to snatch a breath.

Cyriac powered up from the floor and his head cracked into Ginsberg's chin, slamming his mouth shut and breaking his jaw. Ginsberg's eyes glazed with pain and he staggered back from his opponent.

Cyriac was merciless, driving those piston-like punches into the sheriff's body. He struck hard and fast without pause. Like a lumberjack working on felling a tree, he went to work, ruthlessly chopping – chopping – chopping.

Feebly Ginsberg tried to close with Cyriac – tried to wrap his big brawny arms around him in an attempt to smother the vicious punishment he was taking. It was like trying to tame a tornado. There was no stopping that stiff-armed rhythmic pummelling – pounding away at his body, shaking Ginsberg to the core of his being, weakening his ability to carry on fighting.

He backed up, looking around desperately for Walbeck to save him – for anyone to rescue him from the terrible punishment he was taking. But there was no help coming. The referee had crawled from the ring and lay slumped on the floor, ignored by everyone as they watched in awed silence the massacre of their unbeatable champion.

Aimee was finding it difficult pushing her way through the

crowded marquee. Anyone who knew her would have had trouble recognizing her as a young woman. She was wearing a spare suit that belonged to Doctor McCullough and carrying a medical bag which she used to push people out of the way. It had been the brainchild of Arlene to dress Aimee as a male so she could get into the fight arena and help Doctor McCullough and Cyriac in any way possible.

'What the hell!' a big man growled, glaring at her.

'I'm a doctor,' Aimee snarled back. 'I'm trying to get through to the ring.'

It seemed to be working as reluctantly the crowd parted and she was allowed to squeeze through the tightly packed throng. There was much grumbling and even threats but she steadily made headway until at last, sweating and dishevelled, she neared the ring.

Eagerly she searched for Doctor McCullough. Aimee was not to know she was at the opposite corner of the ring to where she would have encountered the doctor. Instead she had arrived at Ginsberg's corner.

'Damn,' she muttered, wondering what to do next.

Aimee hovered, indecisive, while around her the crowd roared like an enraged animal as the action in the ring fired up once more. She rose on her tiptoes and was able to get a clear view of the ring. Her eyes opened wide as she viewed the action.

Cyriac was pounding the sheriff, who was reeling as if drunk around the ring. At last he made it to the ropes directly opposite Aimee and clung there, pleading for help while his body took more punishment from a relentless Cyriac.

Aimee looked to where the big man was directing his pleas and immediately recognized the men who had arrested and pistol-whipped Turlough. She stepped back a

99

pace, not wanting them to see her and possibly recognize her as an accomplice of the condemned man.

The deputies were conferring with great urgency, for it was obvious their boss was being slowly pounded into defeat. She tensed as she saw one of them draw a pistol and his companions closed in around him. Aimee stood irresolute as the men conferred. They came to some conclusion; they broke apart and started brawling.

Spectators scattered from the melee when the deputies pulled weapons and brandished them in the air. Aimee knew immediately what was about to happen. In the confusion, one of the deputies would fire at Cyriac. Ginsberg couldn't stop him – but a bullet would.

## 22

The big lawman clung to the ropes, bawling for someone to help him, his broken jaw making his blubbering incomprehensible. Walbeck, the referee, the only one who might have come to his aid, had crawled from the ring and was lying in the dirt, a broken man.

Cyriac tried to pull his opponent around to get a proper punch at him, but Ginsberg was clinging to the ropes like a drowning man to a floating log. In the end Cyriac gave up the effort and concentrated on pummelling the human punch bag.

Ginsberg, who had wrought similar damage on every man who had ever came against him, killing several in the course of his career, was now being served up his own brand of brutal fighting.

A demon had taken over Cyriac and he was solely intent on demolishing this giant of a man who had sought to ruin him and his friends. With the red haze colouring his world, Cyriac set to work with dedication and with each punch, Ginsberg grew weaker.

Down below him, unbeknownst to Cyriac, a rescue plan was underway to save the besieged lawman. Under cover of his brawling companions, Deputy Jesse Linenan was waiting for a clear shot at Cyriac. He could see his boss visibly weakening as he hung on the ropes, helpless against the savage pounding of his opponent. Their instructions had been plain. On no account could Sheriff Ginsberg lose this match. Not that anyone doubted the outcome of the fight. That was, not until now. Once it became clear that Ginsberg was in trouble, Elwood Black had issued his orders.

'Kill that bastard! Whatever it takes!'

And now the plan was going into action.

Aimee was beside the group of deputies when the row kicked off. Using her doctor's satchel like a battering ram, she worked her way into the mêlée.

'Make way there,' she yelled. 'Let me through. I'm a doctor.'

She had a good idea what was going on and who was to fire the fatal shot, and watched the deputy as he hovered about with a gun in hand, his whole attention on the fighters. She shunted a man away and was rewarded with an elbow in the ribs. Undaunted, she kicked him and he howled and got out of her way. Someone cannoned into her and she went down on her knees. She powered up, crashing into another brawler and got a knee in the side.

'Damn you, puffed up lobos,' she yelled. 'Get the hell outta my way.'

Undaunted by the buffeting she was taking, the bogus doctor was making progress, getting nearer and nearer to Jesse Linenan who was watching for the opportunity to put a bullet in Cyriac. Up in the ring, Cyriac stepped to one side of his victim, punching into a different area of the sheriff's anatomy.

Linenan saw his chance and raised his weapon, his whole attention on Cyriac. It would be an easy shot. A distance of thirty feet or so separated the shooter and target. Linenan was a crack shot; one of the attributes that had brought him to the attention of Ginsberg. A bullet into the Greek's head, then drop back into the anonymity of his brawling companions, no one the wiser as to who had fired the fatal shot.

His hand came up. Someone thumped him in the side as he pulled the trigger and the gun went off target. Instead of hitting Halkias, the bullet punched a hole in Ginsberg's temple, the impact jerking the sheriff's head back. Blood and brains erupted from the rear of the lawman's head.

Linenan's side was hurting like hell. He turned around to look and a young man in a suit was standing beside him, grinding something into his side. There was blood on the newcomer's hand.

'Howdy, Deputy,' Aimee said.

Linenan started to bring the gun around to deal with this threat, but the young man pulled the knife from his side and stuck it in his throat. Linenan opened his mouth to yell but blood bubbled from his lips. The deputy was sinking to the floor and around him the world was growing dim. Aimee stepped back, slipping the bloodied knife back into her doctor's bag.

The crowd panicked as the gunshot was heard. Men were yelling and pushing – attempting to get away from the gunplay. Pandemonium reigned as the panic spread and men were fighting to move away from danger.

Up in the ring, Cyriac sensed the difference in Ginsberg as the man went slack. He stepped back, ready to deliver the *coup de grâce*. Then he noticed the blood.

The sheriff stayed upright, his arms draped over the rope, rigidly clasping them in a death grip. Cyriac's bloodied fists dropped to his sides as he stared uncomprehendingly at Ginsberg. He noticed a young man in a suit clambering into the ring, throwing a bag ahead of him. Then Doctor McCullough was at his side, taking his arm and pulling him away.

'Cyriac, come away. Come with me.'

Cyriac allowed the doctor and the young man to guide him across the ring, the rage and fight leaking from him like a burst water bag. There was something familiar about the youngster helping the doctor but Cyriac couldn't figure out where he had seen him before.

They hassled and pushed an unresisting Cyriac out of the ring, through the milling crowd and got him back to the cubical. The real doctor and the bogus one chivvied the dazed man into his clothes and then pulled him along towards one of the exits.

It was a mad scramble, for everyone had the same idea – to get out of the marquee before they were caught up in the violence now erupting in different sections of the crowd.

The throng spilled out into the open like steers out of a corral and the three escapees were jettisoned into daylight along with them. Then they were hurrying through the town, keeping their grip on a dazed and compliant Cyriac. Arlene was holding the door open for them as they pushed through.

'Cyriac,' she said, her hand to her mouth as she saw his bloody and bruised face.

He tried to smile and fell flat on his face.

## 23

Elwood Black was in his suite in the Green Baize Hotel holding court. The men with him were the deputies of the now deceased Sheriff Ginsberg.

'What the goddamn hell do I pay you guys for? One lousy bum fighter and you can't take care of him. What the hell went wrong? You all know Ginsberg was a certainty to win that fight. He never lost a bout yet. Hell, you couldn't get odds against him. Now he's dead. Shot in the head by, I suspect, that clay-brained whoreson Linenan. God job he's dead too or I might be tempted to send him to Boot Hill anyway.

'Where the hell am I gonna get a new fighter from? Ginsberg was a cash cow. He drew crowds from all over the country. With every fight we were guaranteed a fortune. We could never get decent odds on him but the fans more than made up for that. What a goddamn mess.'

Black kicked a chair and it skidded across the floor, cracking into the shins of the unfortunate fella in the way. The men in the room were subdued and cowed.

'This day's work has cost me dear. Doctor McCullough holds a note for ten thousand dollars that I never expected to have to pay out. I lost a prime fighter and a sheriff along with a deputy, not that Linenan is much of a loss.

'I want that Greek rooster dead,' Black continued in a quieter tone. 'I don't care how it's done. I don't want him collecting on that note nor getting his hands on Benedict's mine.' He paused in his ranting. 'Benedict! I guess we'll have to kill him, too. I suggest some of you take him out in the morning and hang him.'

'Wait a moment, boss,' Trent Masterson spoke up, 'just think on it. With Ginsberg gone and Linenan dead too, we ain't got us a sheriff or chief deputy to take on a hanging. Folk were afraid of Ginsberg. He kept people in line. With him gone, you might have a mite of trouble on your hands if you go hanging Benedict without Ginsberg to scare off anyone as objects.'

Black glowered at the deputy and nodded slowly.

'Hell, maybe you're right. Too many things have gone wrong lately. Perhaps it might be better if you took Benedict out somewhere, well away from town, and finish him off. Try and make it look like an accident.'

Masterson hitched his gun belt higher and smiled confidently. 'I won't let you down, boss. Can I take Ken with me?' The deputy indicated a thin, pale-faced individual with restless eyes standing behind him.

'Take whoever you like. Just make sure you do the job right.'

When they came for Turlough he was a mess – his face was covered in dried blood. He groaned audibly when the deputies grabbed his arms and hauled him to his feet.

'Come on, fella, look lively. We're going for a little ride.'

Turlough mumbled incoherently and sagged when they let go of him. He did feel bad but a lot of it was simulated. He had an inkling of what the lawmen were up to.

'Hell, damn it, can't you walk?'

Turlough promptly sank to the floor and hung his head between his knees, groaning continuously.

'Linenan sure made a good job of softening him up. He was a cruel bastard, was Jesse. Now he's crow bait. I wonder who it was stuck that knife in him. I know we all hated him so it could have been anyone.' Masterson kicked Turlough. 'We're gonna have to carry the son of a bitch.'

'Hell, I ain't carrying him,' Ken said. 'If we take an arm apiece we can lug him outside.'

They dragged the helpless youngster from the cell through the jail and out the back door.

'One of us should fetch the horses. That way no one will see us hauling this piece of shit around and put two and two together when they find his body.'

'Ken, I knew there was a reason I asked for your help. You got a good head on those shoulders. Toss a coin to see who goes for the horses.'

Turlough knew he had to make his move soon. When he heard his captors were to split up he realized there might be a chance of him surviving. He groaned and clasped his hands to his stomach, getting a grip on the knife hidden under his shirt.

A few days ago when Cyriac and the sisters had visited him, Aimee had leaned over him, gloating at his predicament. The deputies had been highly amused as she told him she would be in the front row to watch him hang. The lawmen laughed uproariously, encouraging Aimee. She had snarled at them to mind their own business. Then she had hit Turlough, knocking him back and pouncing on him. He yelled for the deputies to get the mad bitch away from him. Under cover of her attack she slid the knife up inside his sleeve.

He was still puzzled how it had come about that a woman who professed an intense dislike for him had aided him in this manner. He wondered if she believed he would be killed attempting to use the knife to escape. Whatever her motive, the time had come to put to good use Aimee's lethal gift.

Masterson lost the toss and left to fetch the horses. Left

alone with the prisoner, the remaining deputy lolled against the back wall of the jail and pulled out the makings. Before he began rolling his smoke, he kicked Turlough a couple of times.

'You know, I'm gonna enjoy killing you,' he remarked. 'I'm gonna ask Trent if I can rough you up some afore throwing you off a cliff. It won't make any difference as you are a mess anyhow. It'll look like you got your injuries in the fall. The same as happened your sister. We threw her in the river to make it look like suicide. A pity she had to die. We had some fun with her afore we killed her.'

There came the flare of a Lucifer as the deputy fired up his smoke. That was when Turlough moved. He came off the floor and drove the knife with all his strength into the neck of his tormentor, the remark about his sister sparking an incandescent rage that added to the viciousness of the attack. The deputy made gurgling sounds as the blade penetrated his neck, severing his windpipe.

'That's a little present from my sister,' Turlough hissed. 'She said, "Roast in hell!"'

Turlough pressed against the dying man as his life's blood splashed over him, adding to the bloodstains already on his face and clothing. When the deputy's struggles ceased, Turlough stepped back and the body sagged to the dirt. He leaned against the wall where moments before, the deputy had casually admitted to murdering his younger sister.

He tried to block out the remark by the dead man about having fun with Lily before they killed her but the awful thought of his innocent sister in the power of these brutes would not be suppressed. Turlough wept with rage and pain and frustration.

Stooping, he searched the body and recovered a pistol and stuffed it in his belt. He would not be taken so easily again. These were not the days when the law could be respected; these were more days of death.

## 24

Cyriac surfaced in a darkened room. He could make out traces of daylight hemming the curtained window. Slowly he got out of bed, feeling the aches and pains in his bruised and battered body. Peering out into the hallway, he could hear voices and immediately recognized where he was. He opened the door to the parlour to find Doctor McCullough along with Arlene and Beth.

'Well, well, well,' the doctor exclaimed, 'our gladiator has returned to the land of the living.'

Arlene rose from her chair and came over to him. 'We were so worried about you. How are you feeling?'

'I feel like a steer that has been poleaxed then mangled in the slaughterhouse and come out the other side, still alive.' He tried to smile but his face was stiff and hurting. 'I have to thank you for rescuing me,' he continued, nodding to the doctor.

'It's Aimee you have to thank,' McCullough said. 'She saved your life and then helped me get you away from that snake pit.'

'Aimee – where is she?'

The doctor gave a slow smile before answering.

'She's sitting out on my porch with a scattergun on her lap, hoping some of Black's bullyboys will show up again.'

Cyriac walked across and sank into a chair. 'What's been going on?'

'When you had Ginsberg on the ropes, pounding the

living daylight outta him, that snake, Linenan, was fixing to put a bullet in you. Fortunately for you, Aimee stuck a knife in him just as he pulled the trigger and he hit Ginsberg instead.'

'I remember now – Ginsberg flopped over like a dead fish. There was blood everywhere but I never figured on a shooting.'

'With Aimee's help I got you outta there pretty sharpish. She just elbowed her way through everyone. I don't believe I could have managed on my own.'

'So why is she on the porch?'

'Yesterday, Black's men came here looking for you. Aimee borrowed my shotgun and put a load over their heads. Some of them might even have caught a pellet or two. Anyway they didn't hang around to argue. Just took off.'

'You are talking about Aimee – Beth's sister?' Cyriac queried, looking over at Beth.

Beth just nodded and then shrugged. 'Aimee has always been ornery, acting like she has a burr in her pants. I often wonder if she would have been better off if she had been born a fella.'

'We women were wondering how we could help,' Arlene said, 'when I had the idea of dressing Aimee in some of Pa's clothes and sending her into the arena to find out how you were faring. Little did I know she would be able to do more than have a look and come back and tell us what was happening.'

Cyriac might have shaken his head in bewilderment, only it was so painful he was trying to keep stationary.

'That was her – the fella as climbed in the ring! I thought he was an official of some kind.'

'She played her part well,' Doctor McCullough said. 'No one suspected her. Now they are looking for that young doctor as the prime suspect for killing Linenan and Ginsberg.'

'What about Turlough – they let him out?'

'We don't know yet. We'll just have to wait and see.'

'Would you like something to eat?' Arlene asked.

'I'll not put you to any bother. I owe you more than I can ever repay.'

'You have repaid us by staying alive. I have some cold pork and along with a loaf I baked yesterday, I could rustle you up something.' Arlene got to her feet. 'Just come in when you are ready.'

Cyriac stood, too. 'I'll go out front and say hello to Aimee.'

When he stepped out on the porch, Aimee was slouched on a rocker, the scattergun resting across her thighs.

'I believe I owe you my life,' he said.

She scowled at him. 'So?'

'So I owe you.'

'So buy me a new hat.'

Even though it hurt his battered face to do so, Cyriac smiled. 'What colour ribbons would you like on it – pink or maybe yeller?'

'I don't want no ribbons, you dumb jerk,' Aimee snarled. 'Forget the hat.'

'I might forget the hat but I won't forget what you did. Miss Arlene is getting me a bite to eat. Won't you join me?

Aimee hawked and spat, not deigning to answer. Still grinning, Cyriac went back inside.


For the second time in less than a month, Turlough found himself hunted. Once his escape was discovered, Clive Carter, Elwood Black's hunting dog, would be after him and Turlough was desperately seeking the means to get away from Gold Point.

He had fled Thomaston immediately on killing the deputy who had confessed to the murder of his sister, but now he was stranded without a horse. The only place he was reasonably familiar with was Gold Point and it was to there he had run.

Right now he was looking down on the diggings and wondering if he could steal a horse. The previous time he had taken flight he had done so on foot and that had ended disastrously. He knew he needed to get as far away as possible, as quickly as possible, and the only way to accomplish that was on the back of a horse. Turlough realized he was only adding to his crimes by horse rustling but he was so far mired in trouble he didn't think he need worry about getting deeper in.

Jake Ortiz ran a livery alongside his mining activities and kept a string of ponies for sale or hire. His business consisted of a ramshackle barn where he stored his feed and tackle. Adjoining this was a corral and from Turlough's vantage point, he could see several horses. There didn't seem to be any activity immediately around the livery but Turlough kept up his vigil for a while more in order to make sure Ortiz was not in the vicinity and concluded the ostler was probably working his claim.

Cautiously, Turlough began his slow descent towards the livery, stopping every now and again to scan the area for signs of activity. No one seemed to be about and Turlough crept the last hundred yards or so without seeing anything to cause alarm.

'Well, at least something is going my way,' he muttered as he neared the corral.

His next thought was whether he should just throw a leg over a mount and ride it bareback or if he should risk grabbing a saddle from the livery barn. In the end he decided not to push his luck.

Once more he paused and listened. Nothing suspicious – nearby the scrape of a shovel on dirt, an axe thudding into a log, shouted instructions, voices raised in argument.

He was at the gate and rather than open it, he climbed over. The dozen or so animals turned idle heads to watch him as he approached. Turlough chose a Mustang he thought looked fairly docile. He looked around for a length of rope to fashion a halter and spied a coiled lariat hung from one of the posts nearest the barn. Moving carefully so as not to spook the animals, Turlough recovered the rope and stepped over to the Mustang.

'Atta, boy,' he said gently, 'you and I are going on a little trip.'

The Mustang edged away, keeping an apprehensive eye on the interloper. Turlough made soothing noises while glancing about to see if he had been discovered. There did not appear to be anyone in sight and Turlough continued his stalking. That was when he heard the distinctive click of a Colt hammer being drawn back. Slowly Turlough turned and saw two men at the fence with pistols pointing squarely at him.

'Well, well! Killer turned horse thief. Pity we can't hang you twice. Once for murder and again for hoss rustling.'

## 25

'I guess it's time to pay a visit to the jailhouse and find out if Black is prepared to honour his part of the deal and release Turlough,' Cyriac said. He glanced over at Beth and Aimee. 'Then we can all return to the cabin – one big happy family.'

Aimee scowled and Cyriac imagined she would have wanted to spit, only they were indoors. Doctor McCullough nodded his approval.

'I'll come with you. It will be interesting to know who Black has appointed to replace Ginsberg.'

'Doc, I don't like you getting involved any more in this. You have already put yourself in danger by helping me at the fight. Maybe you should lie low for the time being.'

'Humph!' the doctor snorted. 'You think I'm afraid of Black and his murderous rogues? They are perfidious dogs, but someone has to stand up to them. Until you came along they believed they were untouchable. Now thanks to you and Aimee, Black has lost his bullyboy sheriff and people might think it's time to stand up to him and his crooked organization. So don't tell me to step easy. I could say the same to you.'

Cyriac shrugged and then winced as his hurts and bruises kicked in, reminding him of his recent battering in the ring with the now dead bruiser, Ginsberg. Aimee and Beth elected to come too, as did Arlene.

There were two horses tied up outside the sheriff's office that looked like they'd just been ridden in, still saddled and lathered up. Sure enough, when the little party entered, they found two deputies in earnest conversation with two strangers. All turned to stare with hostile eyes at the newcomers. Cyriac noted the tied down holsters of the four men and concluded these were some of Black's enforcers. He wasted no time on introductions.

'I've come to collect a prisoner you are holding here, Benedict Turlough.'

The four men split apart and hands crept to rest on gun butts.

'And who the hell do you think you are, busting in here and demanding prisoners released?' Trent Masterson growled.

'You know who I am. You were one of Linenan's side-kicks. I had an agreement with Black that Benedict would be released as part of a deal we made if I fought Sheriff Ginsberg. I kept my part of the arrangement so now I expect Black to honour his commitment and release Benedict.'

'So this is the tough guy that shot Sheriff Ginsberg,' a gunman with a broken nose that had never been set properly, sneered.

'Yeah, that's right,' Cyriac replied evenly. 'I had a Colt .45 hidden in my drawers. With hundreds of people watching I pulled that gun and shot Ginsberg from behind right in the forehead. Now we cleared that up, will you release Benedict?'

'Can't say as I can do that,' said the second deputy, a burly looking man with a broad, cruel looking face. 'Come to think on it, maybe we ought to arrest you for the murder of Sheriff Ginsberg.'

For long, hard moments the tension in the room mounted as the men calculated the odds of four of them against a single man backed by three females and the doctor. Black had ordered that Halkias was to be killed and they could see no reason why the four of them could not do the deed there and then.

Cyriac was wondering how to defuse the situation when he sensed moment beside him. He daren't take his eyes off the four gunmen so it was with some surprise to perceive Aimee step up beside him and heft the scattergun. He had not realized she had carried it under her coat. But then she was so shapeless it was no wonder he hadn't unnoticed. With characteristic gaucheness, she hawked and spat in the direction of the four men, edgy and ready to explode into action.

'I guess I can take two of these polecats with this here scattergun,' she stated. 'You figure you can take the other two? I hit the whoresons on the left and you take out the pieces of buffalo dung on the right.'

For a moment it looked touch and go but slowly fingers slackened and hands surreptitiously slid away from holstered weapons and Cyriac relaxed.

'Now we cleared the air, let's cut the playing around and release Benedict.'

Masterson smirked. 'Like I said, I can't do that.'

Cyriac made an effort to curb his anger. 'Do I have to go to Black and tell him you won't honour his agreement?'

'You can tell Mr Black what the hell you like. I can't release Benedict because he ain't here. He killed a deputy and broke outta here last night.'

'The hell you say? More 'an likely you dung beetles took him out and murdered him.'

The deputy's smirk grew wider, as did that of his companions.

'No, he's still alive. Ain't that right, boys?'

Their own smirks became bigger as their confidence soared for restoring the advantage in their own favour.

'I can tell you where that murdering piece of shit is at.'

'Yeah?'

Cyriac's unease was growing. There was something too smug about these gunnies. They were obviously gloating over something that boded badly for Benedict.

'He's a guest of Mr Black out at his mine.'

Cyriac's eyes narrowed at this news. 'You telling me Black is so fond of Benedict he has him as his houseguest?'

The men were sniggering, enjoying baiting Cyriac.

'Well, you see, after he broke outta jail and murdered Deputy Ken Widnes, he thought to go out to the mine and murder Mr Black.

115

'Fortunately he was captured before he could carry out his plan. So that's where your murdering no good Benedict is. We got him penned up at the mine. I can tell you now he may not leave there alive. Mr Black's miners are riled up some and wanted to string him up there and then. That's where these two rannies have come from now.' Masterson indicated the two gunmen. 'They were the ones as captured him.'

## 26

Cyriac lay on the hill and trained his eyeglass on the mine workings. The site was extensive and he watched as pipes hosed tons of water into the cuttings, washing out gravel and rocks in huge quantities. Men worked at the bottom as the waste was flushed, dredging and loading it into mule drawn wagons.

Even from his high vantage point, the roar of the driven water sounded loud, as the jets generated a fearsome force sufficient to wash out the gold bearing gravel. Cyriac watched for some time, noting the armed guards placed at intervals around the site and the number and position of the various buildings, trying to identify their purpose and how frequently they were used by the men operating the site.

There was no sign of Turlough, not that Cyriac expected to be able to see him. If what the deputies had said were true, they would have Turlough securely locked up. And then he noticed the outhouse and the man who sat outside with a Winchester across his knees. He studied the place for a while and came to the conclusion the man was on sentry duty, guarding something or someone inside the shack. When he first mooted the idea of going out to Black's mine, he met a hail of protests from his companions.

'You can't go out to that place,' Doctor McCullough protested. 'It'll be a suicide trip. They have armed guards patrolling twenty-four hours. Black is very jealous of his mine workings. A while back some of his rivals tried to sabotage the pumps used to propel the water jets. He sent Clive Carter after them and rumour has it none of those men survived.'

'Turlough mentioned this Carter fella when I first came across him. Said it was Carter as was hunting him.'

'Carter is a deadly snake. He's wanted for murder in several states, but Black gives him sanctuary out at the mine. There are those who believe Carter and his gang of killers carry out robberies and killings in different parts of the country and then return to hide out at the mine. It is well known that when Black wants some serious killing done he unleashes Carter.'

'And the law don't do nothing about it?'

'Humph! Black is the law as you should know. He appoints the sheriff and administers his own brand of justice.'

'How do you know those men were telling the truth about Turlough?' Arlene asked. 'It might be a ploy to lure you out there and finish what they failed to do at the fight.'

'I have a feeling they were telling the truth. They were too smug while they were telling the tale. No.' Cyriac shook his head. 'I'm convinced they've got him all right.'

In the face of their protests he had assured them he was not going to the mine to take any action but only to spy out the land. Beth and Aimee decided to accompany him part of the way as they were anxious to return to the Benedict cabin.

Cyriac rolled on his back and went over all he had seen. It seemed an impossible task to get down into what was essentially an armed camp. It was a problem Cyriac was determined to crack.

Down there, protected by Black's wealth, were the men who had caused the death of Milo. Cyriac wanted to seek out those men and exact the ultimate penalty for the slaying of his brother.

He rode back to Gold Point, much preoccupied with the problems he must surmount to get into Black's mine workings and locate Turlough. The women were anxious to quiz him when he arrived back at the shack. He told them he needed more time to reconnoitre. Then he went out front and sat on the step of the porch and stared across the diggings, thinking of Black and how he was gouging out the riches of the earth. Though he had plenty of scope to work his own patch, he still coveted the diggings of Gold Point and if that meant killing the people who stood in his way, that was of no consequence.

Cyriac wondered how many had died as a result of Black's greed. His brother Milo was one victim and then according to Doctor McCullough, there was Arlene's fiancé Robert as well as Turlough's sister Lily. He sighed deeply and went inside and retrieved his saddle bags and began his preparations. Knives and guns – a man could never have too many killing devices.

Cyriac sat down and began to hone his big Bowie knife. Blades were silent and deadly. He worked steadily on the big blade, polishing and honing until he was satisfied with its edge. While Beth prepared a meal, Aimee sat opposite and observed everything he did.

Guns next. Mook Holdout revolver, Remington New Model revolver, Starr Army .44, Smith & Wesson. Breaking them down and rubbing in the oil. Checking the mechanism. And finally loading them from boxes of ammunition.

'Looks like you aim to fight a war with all that hardware,' Aimee commented.

The only response from Cyriac was the raising of eyebrows.

'What you aim to do?' Aimee persisted.

If she expected an explanation she was disappointed for all she got from Cyriac was a shrug.

'You gotta have a plan,' she persisted.

'I ride in there, shoot a few of Black's men, find Turlough and ride back out again.'

'You'll need help.'

'I'm best when I'm on my own. That way I don't have to worry about any fellow travellers.'

Aimee got up and fetched an old revolver and the scattergun she had appropriated from Doctor McCullough, and borrowing Cyriac's cleaning equipment, started working on the weapons.

'You'll need help,' she repeated as she toiled.

'I just told you: I work best on my own.'

'So I needn't have bothered to stop Linenan from shooting you when you were fighting Ginsberg. You would have climbed out of the ring, put down Linenan and his buddies and then jumped back into the ring and finished off Ginsberg.'

Cyriac stared long and hard at Aimee who kept her head down, engrossed in her work.

'I ain't denying you saved my life back there, but this is different. Black's mine is an armed camp. He has gunmen dotted all around the site. Anyone trying to get in there is a likely target for a dozen or more riflemen. There is a strong possibility anyone attempting to crash in there will not survive.'

Aimee raised her head and stared him straight in the eye. 'Then why are you proposing to do just that?'

'Damn it all, woman, risking my own life is not the same as putting someone else in danger.' Cyriac stood. 'So just you stay here and look after your sister.'

'Ain't no use you telling me what to do. I'll just follow you anyway. You need someone to watch your back.'

The pair glowered at each other, neither giving an inch.

' "It is better to dwell in the corner of the housetop than with a contentious woman in a wide house",' Cyriac quoted.

Aimee was not to be bested. 'Like a lame man's legs which are useless,' she said, 'so is a proverb in the mouth of foolish men—'

'You might as well get used to it,' Beth cut in. 'Aimee is a law on to herself. Once she decides to do something then nothing on God's earth will stop her. If you want to keep her out of any action you are planning, you'll have to hogtie her and set an armed guard to watch her.'

## 27

Cyriac critically examined Aimee. She wore grimy work overalls and her face was smudged with charcoal. A dilapidated hat hid her long hair.

'Well?' she scowled at him as she spoke.

'You'll terrify the children if they catch sight of you in

that getup,' he replied, trying not to smile.

'Good, I hate kids.'

'Can you drive a wagon?' he asked.

'Sure, I can drive a wagon. Any idiot can handle a wagon.'

'Come and have a look,' he said and went outside.

A covered wagon was parked by the side of the cabin. If Aimee looked grubby and unkempt, the wagon was the perfect vehicle for her. The cover was made from decaying skins that were full of holes and certainly wouldn't keep out any amount of weather. The wagon itself was no better with a few bust planks here and there. There was even a spoke or two missing from the wheels.

'Your chariot, my princess.' Cyriac waved a hand towards the crate.

'Holy flyblown cadavers, do you expect me to drive that disaster? It looks as if it wouldn't be fit to dump in the desert. Or is that where you found it?'

'Hell, I paid twenty dollars for that rig, so don't be turning your nose up at it. With a bit of luck it will get us into Black's mine.'

'Twenty dollars! By heck, they must have seen you coming! I'd o' thought they'd pay you to take it off their hands.' Aimee hawked and spat in the direction of the wagon, scoring a hit on a wheel. 'I take it you got a plan?'

'Do you smoke?' Cyriac asked.

Aimee looked away and spat again. 'Sometimes.'

For answer, Cyriac went to the wagon and uncovered a box with red lettering on the lid: EXPLOSIVES! DO NOT SMOKE! And to emphasize the warning, a skull and cross-bones accompanied the writing. Opening the box, he took out a cylinder about eight inches long and as fat as a beeswax candle. A short fuse projected from one end.

'Just so you know what you are getting into,' Cyriac said

121

and turned around, holding the stick and found he was alone. The door of the shack slammed closed. 'What the hell!' Cyriac put the dynamite back in the box and covered it over.

Inside the shack he found Aimee and Beth sitting at the table. Aimee had taken off her hat and her hair hung down, covering her face. Cyriac went to the stove and poured coffee into three mugs, took them over and sat down. Aimee kept her head lowered and would not look at him.

'Aimee,' he said gently, 'you have every right to be scared of dynamite.'

'I ain't scared!' she snapped, still not looking up.

'That's all right. Seeing as you were so hell-bent on accompanying me, it never occurred to me you might object to driving a wagonload of dynamite. I'm glad I found out afore we set out. I don't want you to feel bad about this. There ain't many as would go near a box of explosives, never mind travel with it in that rattletrap outside.'

'What you gonna do?' Beth asked.

'Do what I do best,' Cyriac answered. He finished his coffee and stood for a moment in deep thought. With a sigh he unfastened a money belt and slung it on the table. 'If anything happens to me there's enough money there to give you both a fresh start in life – somewhere away from here – more civilized. Give a share of it to Doc McCullough.'

He turned abruptly and went outside. As he walked around the wagon, the door of the shack opened and Aimee appeared. Without saying a word, she climbed up into the driver's seat.

'Aimee!'

'Shut the hell up!'

'I was just going to tell you I'll be in the back of the wagon under a buffalo hide. Your job is to get us past any guards as might be patrolling. Tell them you're looking for work – anything on offer. Once the shooting starts, get under the wagon and stay there.'

As soon as he was aboard, Aimee started up the team and the wagon rattled and lurched through the camp. Cyriac opened the box marked with the skull and crossbones and carefully pushed several sticks inside his pockets. He placed some on the floor. Then he lay back and pulled the decrepit buffalo robe up to his chin. From this position he could see the sky through the holes in the wagon's covering. The lurching and swaying of the vehicle almost sent him to sleep and then he could hear Aimee calling to him.

'I can see the mine up ahead.'

'Yeah!' he called back. 'Keep her rolling.'

He eased the Remington from the holster and held it ready. The wagon rumbled on. Soon he could hear the geysers. They pumped water twenty-four hours. He breathed deeply.

This is what I do best, he told Beth. And it was true. He was a killer and he was walking into a den of killers equally vicious and callous. There would be no quarter – no mercy on either side. It was kill or be killed. Men would die and blood would flow. Some of the blood might be his and today he faced death. Well, he had faced death on many occasions in the past.

The Keres – the female spirits of death – were close. He could sense their presence, imagined he could feel the wind from the beating of their wings. They came to him at times like this. It was his fate to be the purveyor of death.

Charon, the ferryman of the Styx, would be waiting to transport the souls of the slain to Hades, the region of the dead. The time of blood and death was imminent, the days of death were nigh.

'Hold up there! Where the hell do you think you are going?' a gruff voice hollered.

'I was told to come out here and I would get work. I can do anything – haulage mainly,' Aimee replied. 'But I'll work in the diggings if needs be.'

'Hell, I don't think they're hiring at the moment.'

'Like my old ma used to say: if you don't ask, you don't get.'

'OK, fella, carry on. But I reckon you'll be wasting your time.'

The wagon jerked into motion again. They were inside the compound. The first part of Cyriac's plan was in place.

## 28

Cyriac sat up inside the wagon and peered through a tear in the cover. He had a mental map of the area from when he surveyed it with his glass.

'Veer right,' he called out to Aimee.

Obediently she hauled on the reins and the wagon changed direction. Now that they were inside the complex, no one took any notice of the shoddy vehicle lumbering through the works. They were heading towards a group of wooden buildings and it was here Cyriac reckoned they were holding Turlough.

He pulled a cigar from his jacket and struck a Lucifer, thinking if Aimee could see what he was doing she might leap from the wagon and start running.

When he had the cigar smouldering well, he picked up a couple of sticks of dynamite and held the cigar to the fuses. Once they caught, he stood at the rear of the wagon and tossed one hard over the top of the wooden shack they were passing. The second one he threw out towards a great heap of spoil.

When the explosion came it ripped the decayed covering from the wagon, leaving Cyriac exposed. The horses tried to buck as the blast swept over them but the heavy wagon kept them in place. By this time they were amongst the cluster of buildings and Cyriac leapt to the ground.

'Get in there!' he yelled at Aimee, pointing underneath the wagon.

She hauled on the brake and leapt down beside him and gave him a tight grin. To his surprise she was clutching the scattergun. Cyriac sensed she wasn't one for hiding under any wagon.

'We gotta look for Benedict. He must be in one of these buildings. Act like you are one of the crew and run about as if you are not sure what is going off. I'll meet you back here.'

She nodded and hurried into the maze of shanties. Before Cyriac could follow, a flurry of shots was fired at him – most hitting the rotten body of the wagon. He turned and kicked in the first door he came to and dived inside.

A couple of men swung around, startled by his dramatic entrance. As Cyriac came through the door they grabbed for their holstered weapons. Cyriac had his Remington in his hand but chose not to fire it. Instead he vaulted across the intervening space and lashed out at one man, catching him on the side of the head with his pistol. He swung his elbow and hit his companion in the temple with enough force to put him down. For a moment he glared down at the men, his weapon pointed and ready to fire.

The cold fire of combat had been lit within him and he could feel the killing urge strong upon him. The men were out of action but it was with a supreme effort of will he stayed his trigger finger. He headed for the rear door and cautiously opening it, peered outside. He saw a group of men milling around, looking for the source of the explosions, and slipped out the door and ran out to join them.

'There's been an accident,' he yelled. 'Some of the nitro went off. I think it came from over there.'

He pointed in the direction from which he had come and not waiting for a response, he ran around a corner, looking for another door to kick in. He did not get far before a door in a shack burst open and men came spilling out in various stages of undress.

'What's happening?' one yelled at Cyriac.

'The place is under attack,' Cyriac panted. 'They're using dynamite on a wrecking spree. Black wants everyone on the alert. He thinks they're trying to rescue that Benedict fella.'

'Wait a minute – I know you. You're the Greek as killed Ginsberg.' Even as he spoke the speaker was grabbing for his gun. 'Kill the bastard!' he yelled.

He got no further as Cyriac clubbed him across the face and he went down with a broken nose and cheekbone. Now the wild cold thing was loose inside Cyriac and nothing could stop his progress. As the man's companions were grabbing for ironware, Cyriac waded in amongst them, kicking and swinging wildly with boots, fists and pistol.

The barrel of the gun crunching on top of a head, the bone giving under the blow, the victim dropping and before he hit the dirt, Cyriac's fist hammering another man in the throat – the man gagging as his oesophagus was crushed.

Kicking a knee and the joint going back at an angle it was not meant to. The injured man opening his mouth to yell and a bone-hard fist slamming into his chin, breaking his jaw and catapulting him over on to his back.

Cyriac did not remember pulling it, but the Bowie was in one hand. A yell as the blade punched into a belly, ripping upwards and blood and guts spilling out. Kicked out of the way and the next obstacle bludgeoned and toppling into the dirt, and then there was no one to hit or stab.

Not pausing to assess the damage he had inflicted, Cyriac ploughed on, rounding a corner and seeing a man with a rifle standing outside a shack, turned towards him and taking in the gun and the bloody knife in the hands of the man coming towards him, brought up his rifle and fired.

The shot was hasty and the bullet passed underneath Cyriac's armpit. He levered another shell into the chamber. Cyriac was running towards the rifleman and snapped off a shot. The bullet took him in the shoulder and he jerked back, trying to fire again but Cyriac got another shot off and the bullet hit him in the eye and he fell backwards, his brains spilling from the puncture in the back of his head.

Cyriac skidded to a stop as he noted the heavy padlock on the door the rifleman had been guarding. Coolly, he shot the padlock, having to use two slugs to do the job. His hammer clicked on empty and he pouched the gun before pulling his Smith & Wesson. Once again he kicked in a door and shouted.

'Turlough, are you in there?'

There was movement inside and a figure stumbled to the door.

'Cyriac, thank God! What's happening?'

For answer Cyriac handed him the Remington along with a handful of shells.

'Here, load that. We're getting outta here.'

As he handed over the weapon, he heard above the noise and confusion of yelling men the sound of a scatter-gun going off. He grabbed Turlough and hauled him outside.

'Come on. That's Aimee if I'm not mistaken. She's in trouble.'

## 29

A crowd was gathered around someone who was the centre of attention. Cyriac, taller than most men, could see over the heads and saw Aimee being held by two burly men. A third man was yelling at her and at the same time punching her. Cyriac fired over the heads of the mob, immediately getting their attention. Some scattered out of the way but others grabbed for guns. Cyriac had no option but to fire into the body of those milling around Aimee.

Two were hit but others had gotten their guns out and began shooting back. Cyriac fanned the Smith & Wesson, knocking down another couple of gunmen. Behind him, Turlough had managed to load the Remington and joined in the shooting.

The man who had been punching Aimee turned his head towards the source of the shooting. It was a mistake to take his attention off his prisoner and she took the opportunity to kick him in the crotch. He folded and sank to the dirt. Aimee started struggling with the men holding her. Seeing their comrades being shot down, they released their captive to grab for weapons.

Aimee seized the man on the right and swung him into his companion, knocking them both off balance. She threw herself at them and the three of them went down in an untidy heap – Aimee kicking and punching the two men in a wild fury. So fierce was her attack they had no chance of getting at their weapons. One of them grabbed Aimee in a chokehold and Aimee stabbed him in the eye with a stiffened finger.

'Aaagh!' he yelled and let go of his hold.

Aimee head butted him and he tried to roll away out of her reach. His companion punched Aimee in the side of the head and she grunted and lashed out with her fist. He grabbed for his pistol and brought it up towards his attacker. He opened his mouth and his eyes widened as he felt the knife go into his side.

'Damn you!' he cursed as he realized what had happened.

Aimee slashed the bloodied knife across the hand that held the gun, almost severing a couple of fingers. He opened his mouth to yell and Aimee stabbed him in the throat with the knife – blood jetting over his shirt. He fell away from her but she scrabbled after him and grabbed the revolver from his unresisting hand.

A figure loomed over her and she swung around, fumbling to get a grip on her newly acquired weapon. Someone yelled at her and she got a look at him. Cyriac was reaching out a hand to her.

'Come on!' he hollered 'We got Turlough.'

She clambered to her feet, wincing as she felt the

bruises where her captors had hit her. Shots were coming in towards them but Cyriac's whirlwind attack had scattered the gunmen and most had fled for cover. He turned and fanned a flurry of shots towards the main group cowering behind a small shack.

'Over there!' he yelled and pointed to a large building.

Cyriac sprinted across the intervening distance and used his usual method of opening doors. His boot splintered the latch and the door crashed open. He took the men within by surprise as he hurtled through the ruined door. They turned towards the intruder, guns at the ready.

As Cyriac came to a halt he fired, hitting two men in the upper body. They staggered back, blood pumping from the bullet wounds. One tried to fire at the intruder but another shot from Cyriac put him down permanently. The others were turning to flee and Cyriac held his fire as they ran to the rear of the building and vanished out of the back door.

He glanced around and realized he was in a warehouse containing tools and machinery. Aimee dashed inside, followed closely by Turlough. Cyriac studied the place for a moment until he spotted what he was looking for.

'How are we to get outta here?' Turlough panted.

'We create a diversion,' Cyriac answered. 'Keep a look out and fire a few shots out the windows and watch the doors.'

He found a pinch bar and jammed it in the lid of a wooden crate. He could hear the sound of breaking glass as Turlough broke out a window and fired through it. Aimee ran to the rear entrance where the men fleeing Cyriac had left and fired out of the open door.

Cyriac overturned the crate he had broken open. A pile of wands very similar to the ones he had initially carried to the mine spilled on to the floorboards. Aimee glanced behind her and froze as she saw the heap of deadly sticks.

'Dear God!' she whispered.

Bullets were hitting in and around the door frame, some coming inside. Any moment Aimee expected a bullet to hit that deadly heap and blow them all to kingdom come. Cyriac seemed indifferent to the gunfire going on all around him and was busy slicing a coil of fuse cord into suitable lengths.

'What the hell are you doing?' Aimee yelled at him.

He bared his teeth at her in a wolfish grin and threw his hands upwards in a gesture of something going up in the air. Then he was busy going around the stores, poking the primed sticks here and there amongst the piled up goods.

'I've run out of bullets,' she called, having to yell as the noise of gunfire increased.

For answer he grabbed a couple of cartons from a shelf and tossed them across to her.

'So have I,' Turlough shouted and Cyriac threw him a box.

When she finished reloading, Aimee glanced up at Cyriac and stopped, her eyes widening as she gaped at him. Cyriac, holding a flaming Lucifer, was calmly igniting the fused sticks of dynamite he had distributed about the building.

'No!' she screamed. 'You bloody mad booger! You'll kill us all!'

Benedict turned to see what was going on.

'What the hell. . . !'

He rushed across and grabbed Cyriac by the arm. 'What are you doing? We're trapped in here and you're fixing to blow us all to smithereens.' Benedict stepped back as Cyriac turned his fiercely blazing eyes upon him. 'You're mad,' Benedict whispered.

'You're not the first to say that and I suppose you won't

be the last.'

Benedict reached out to grab the fizzing piece of fuse and then stopped as he became aware of, not one, but myriad little sparks, like fiendish eyes winking at him from amongst the shelves.

'What have you done?' he moaned. 'You've condemned us all to death.'

## 30

Bullets were hammering at the building as the forces outside rallied and more and more gunmen came up to join the fight. Some lead penetrated the windows and the open door where Aimee was valiantly trying to keep the shooters at bay.

'We're in a death trap,' she shouted to no one in particular.

Suddenly Cyriac was beside her, his half-consumed cigar clamped in his mouth still smouldering.

'Keep firing,' he yelled in her ear. 'And then be ready to make a run for it.'

She stared fascinated at the clutch of dynamite sticks clasped in his hand. Without exception they all had very short fuses. One was already lit. Aimee was spellbound as she watched the little tendril of smoke drifting into the air from the fuses. She had never been this close to death ever. She could not speak – could not move. Cyriac elbowed her in the ribs.

'Goddamn it, keep firing.'

She broke from her terror-induced trance and did what he ordered – firing out through the open door.

'Turlough, over here!' Cyriac yelled. He waited till the youngster hunkered down beside him. 'Once I start running, you two follow pronto. Don't hang about. Just keep on my tail.'

Turlough, like Aimee, could not take his eyes from the smoking doom in Cyriac's hand. Using the glowing end of the cigar, he sparked life into two more sticks. He grinned at them, the cigar still in his mouth, and then sprang out the door, his hand coming up, hurling the deadly charge in the direction of the men shooting at them. Twice more he threw and then he was running and behind him, Turlough and Aimee scrambled out of the door after him.

The explosions thundered out somewhere to the rear and they felt the air being sucked from around them. Debris rained down and Aimee stumbled and almost went down. Turlough yelled but could not hear his own words. Something was wrong with his hearing. Ahead he could see Cyriac.

'Wait for us,' he tried to shout but couldn't hear his own voice.

Before he had taken another step, a hot breath of some hellish monster blew suddenly upon him and an irresistible force smote him on the back and he found himself on the ground eating dust. Objects were raining down upon him, some striking him and others ploughing into the dirt.

Someone grabbed his shirt and hauled him to his feet. He looked to see it was Cyriac. He had an arm around Aimee and was pulling her along with him. She shook him off and continued under her own steam.

The air was filled with dust and Turlough could not see where they were going but doggedly kept Cyriac in sight and followed, putting one foot in front of the other, determined not to be left behind.

As they ran, Cyriac would pause and toss another of those deadly sticks into a building or at a piece of machinery or anything that was still standing. On they ran, hearing those mind numbing explosions relentlessly following them as Cyriac left a trail of destruction behind.

A guard carrying a rifle loomed up before them and seeing them running, shouted something. Cyriac shot him as they ran, the gunman buckling at the knees and sinking into the dirt. Suddenly they were clear of buildings and Cyriac paused only long enough to make sure there was no one after them. He led them through rough, boulder strewn hillocks until he turned right and they entered a shallow coulee.

Turlough was breathing hard, hardly able to keep moving, staggering along, only kept upright by sheer willpower and the fear of what lay behind them.

Ahead of him Cyriac slowed to a walk. Kneeling on the ground, he pulled his remaining dynamite sticks from where he had stored them in his pockets and built a pyramid with them. He rolled large rocks to his construction, piling them around until the deadly stack was hidden. Taking his cigar, he lit the end of a long fuse. As he straightened up he grinned at Turlough.

'There is an underground lake beneath this. That is where Black draws his water from to keep his hoses working. I'm hoping when this goes off it might either block it or divert the water so he won't be able to use it anymore. Anyway, after today it will take him a while to get his operation working again.'

He turned and began walking. Turlough cast a nervous glance towards the smoking fuse and imagined the explosives going off and the rocks Cyriac had piled around them being thrown up into the air and crashing down upon anyone in the vicinity. He forgot his weariness and hurried after Aimee and Cyriac. As they climbed out of the gorge, Turlough tensed when he saw horses with a rider atop one.

'Beth,' he said hoarsely.

Beth was mounted on one horse and was holding the leads to three spare mounts. Cyriac strode over to the horses and pulled a rifle from the scabbard.

'Turlough, grab a weapon,' he called. 'We still got some work to do. Aimee, help Beth hold the horses. They'll more than likely spook when that charge goes off.'

Beth handed a rifle to Turlough. 'I'm glad you're safe,' she said, giving him a strained smile.

'You don't know how glad I am to see you,' he rejoined, and really meaning it.

'Come on,' Cyriac exclaimed. 'They'll be here any minute.'

He ran over to the rim and crouched down, rifle held ready. Turlough hurried to join him. They could see the little cairn hiding the deadly charge of dynamite. Sure enough, men carrying rifles came into view, hurrying up the gorge after the fugitives. Cyriac fired off a round. The men scattered and went to ground.

'Don't worry about hitting anyone. We just got to keep them pinned down until that damned charge goes off.'

Turlough triggered a couple of shots. There was sporadic firing from the men down in the gorge, nothing coming very near. Turlough popped his head up to fire at the gunmen and ducked down again. Cyriac emptied his magazine into the gorge, spraying the shots in a wide arc. As his rifle clicked on empty he eased back from the rim.

'Come on, time to go.'

Cyriac ran to the horses and grabbing the reins from Beth, swung aboard.

135

'Go! Go! Go!' he yelled.

Turlough scrambled on top of a grey mare and hauled on the reins, and soon all four horses were racing away from the gorge.

The explosion when it came was muffled and Turlough risked a glance behind. He could see a cloud of dust boiling out of the gorge and shuddered to think of the men who had taken refuge there. There wouldn't be much of them left to bury and he wondered briefly if any of them had been involved in the murder of his sister, Lily.

# 31

'We better steer clear of Thomaston for a few days and let things cool off a mite,' Cyriac told his companions.

'Surely now we gave them that whopping Black will back off,' Turlough said.

They were in Turlough's cabin drinking coffee while discussing their future plans.

'Men like Black don't back off,' Cyriac said. 'He's called the shots in this part of the world for so long he won't let go that easy. There is too much at stake. We must prepare for when he makes his mind up to come after us. Black is like a wolf. He'll attack at our weakest point and that will be any one of us he finds alone. He'll come at us when we least expect it. That means we must be on guard at all times – day and night. We'll draw up a rota and take turns – starting tonight.'

Turlough glanced around at the others. 'That's a

helluva call,' he said. 'There are only four of us.'

Cyriac pressed on relentlessly. 'It's a matter of survival. Make no mistake about it – Black will come after us. We got to be ready when he does come. Four hour shifts.' Cyriac paused as a thought occurred to him. 'Perhaps the womenfolk might want to go somewhere safe until this business is over?'

Aimee scowled at him. 'I ain't going nowhere, but I don't want no more truck with no more blasted dynamite. My ears are still buzzing.'

Except for Beth, they were filthy after their exploits at Black's mine – their faces and clothing grimy and coated with dust.

'I think we will be safe for a day at least, though it won't take Black long to figure out who wrecked his mine,' Cyriac observed. 'Once he discovers Turlough missing, it won't be hard to deduce who is responsible. He might play it shrewd and allow us time to relax and let down our guard. One night when we are sleeping – whoosh – our cabin goes up in flames and as we tumble from our burning bunks, he has a ring of marksmen surrounding the place and picks us off one by one as we stumble out into the cool night air.'

It was a horrific picture Cyriac painted and his companions looked suitably sombre as they thought over his words.

'We could scarper,' Turlough suggested tentatively. 'Get away somewhere and start afresh. We're never gonna beat Black. He'll just keep sending more and more gunmen after us. We can't be on our guard at all times. Eventually he'll get lucky or he'll just bide his time and take us one at a time.'

'Sure,' Cyriac said. 'Go ahead and run. Look where it got you last time. Black sent his pack of wolves after you. My brother, Milo, died because you ran. How far will you get this time?'

'Hell, there's California. I could lose myself amongst the goldfields there.'

'Go ahead. Climb on one of those horses and take off.'

Now that it was put so bluntly Turlough looked uncertain. He stood up.

'Afore you go,' Cyriac said. 'I need you to sign your claim over to me and if the womenfolk want a share then we'll stay put and start panning.'

'How can you talk about working the claim when Black is out there gunning for you?'

Cyriac shrugged. 'You think all life stops because hardnosed men like Black plan to take over the world. Boot Hill is filled with guys like that. Someday a harder dude will turn up and Black in turn will be pushed to one side.'

Looking disgruntled, Turlough sat again. 'I guess I owe you – and Aimee,' he muttered.

'You owe me nothing,' Aimee sneered, 'you gutless sack of guano.'

Ignoring the insult, Turlough looked across at Beth. 'And you, Beth.' Slowly he gazed at each one in turn. 'In fact, I owe you all. In spite of what you think of me, Aimee, you did slip me that blade back in the jail. Without that I would be dead.'

Both Cyriac and Beth turned and looked at Aimee.

'You what?' Beth said.

The big woman's face distorted into her habitual scowl.

'I was hoping he would cut his throat with it.'

'Methinks Aimee hides a heart of gold beneath that harsh exterior,' Turlough said.

'That's how you escaped,' Cyriac said, nodding thoughtfully. 'It just goes to show there are more ways of skinning a cat than rubbing its fur the wrong way.'

'Anyhow, Aimee, you did me a favour. The deputy I killed

was boasting how he and his buddies . . .' The youngster's voice faltered and he stared down at the table for a moment before he could continue. 'He boasted they did things to Lily afore they murdered her. I guess that made it easier for me to stick that knife in him.'

His companions were silent as they took in his words. It was Beth who broke the silence.

'How horrible. What sort of men are we dealing with?'

'Cruel, ruthless men who can kill and torture without conscience or remorse,' Cyriac said. 'Now you know why I am telling you we must be vigilant at all times or go somewhere safe.'

However, when Black struck, it was at their soft unprotected underbelly – a true act of perfidy, well thought out and befitting a man with his animal cunning.

A couple of days later, it was Turlough's turn to stand watch. They were using an abandoned wagon which they dragged up to the summit of a low hill. From there, under cover, they could watch the activity going on around them and spot anything that might hint of an attack. A rider drew up at the cabin and sat his horse. Cyriac, who had been digging in the Benedict claim, recognized the owner of the dry goods store.

'Howdy, Mr Richards, good of you to visit. Will you step down and share a coffee? Won't be as good as that brew your own wife makes but it is all I can offer.'

Cyriac sensed the sombre mood of the man as he nodded his acceptance.

'Thank you, I'd like that.'

'Go on in. I'll join you when I've cleaned up a bit.'

Cyriac rinsed his hands and face in a bucket on the porch and came inside, wiping his hands on a cotton towel.

'Where are your companions?' Richards asked as Cyriac

139

poured coffee.

'Oh, they're around somewhere,' Cyriac answered vaguely, not wanting to give too much away until he knew the reason for the storekeeper's visit.

'Mr Halkias, I got some bad news for you.'

Richards put his hands across his face and stayed like that for a long time. Cyriac waited. He had a sudden premonition of what was coming.

'Elwood Black sent me,' the storekeeper said at last, raising his face and looking at his host. He had a haunted look about him as he spoke. 'At first I refused – so he had his men take my wife as hostage. Told me he would sell her to a cathouse if I didn't do as he said.' His voice broke then and he took a moment to compose himself. 'I believed him. He is the very devil incarnate.' Richards wiped at his eyes before continuing. 'I am to tell you he has Doctor McCullough and his daughter Arlene as guests at the hotel. He invites you to join them.'

## 32

Cyriac rode slowly, his scarred face impassive. He rode through the Gold Point diggings, past the hastily erected wooden shacks and tents that were the only shelter for desperate miners hoping to strike it rich and move into a life of luxury. Past the untidy spoil heaps, the mounds of trash scattered by scavenging dogs, empty cans, bottles, papers, scraps of old garments all mixed together like a statement of the various hopes of the men who worked ceaselessly, digging in the dirt like the human version of prairie dogs.

Some miners looked up from their tasks and called a greeting which Cyriac did not acknowledge. Others ignored him, intent only on grubbing in the earth, eagerly watching for that glimmer of colour that would buy them a night of indulgence amongst the fleshpots of Thomaston.

Cyriac knew as he rode into Thomaston he was under surveillance. Black would have men watching his movements. He would want to know what company he was bringing with him. But Cyriac rode alone. They would know he was coming and that he was coming alone.

He had lied to Turlough and Aimee, telling them Black wanted him, and only him to come, otherwise the vindictive mine owner might be spurred into doing something rash like hurting his hostages. He could see the building anger in Aimee's eyes as she reluctantly accepted his pleas to go into town alone.

'It's the only way,' he insisted. 'As soon as Black has me he'll release the doctor and Arlene and Mrs Richards. He only wants me. You hang on here and stay safe. If anything happens to me you will have to leave Gold Point like Turlough suggested and hightail it to California.'

'He's gonna kill you,' Aimee insisted. 'Black ain't inviting you into Thomaston to have supper with him. As soon as he has you in his power he'll let loose his animal friends on you and they will kill you. Have you thought of that?'

Cyriac had seemed engrossed in checking his weapons and had not responded.

'What's the point of all those knives and guns? He will strip them from you. There's no way he'll allow you to get near him armed.'

'There was this guy called Samson,' Cyriac said softly. 'His weapon was his great strength which he lost when his enemies, the Philistines, shaved his hair off. They were so

141

full of their own cunning they did not reckon on his hair growing back. Once that happened he regained his great strength and was then able to slay his foes.'

'Yeah, I know that story, but didn't Samson die along with them?'

Now Cyriac rode into Thomaston, knowing he was going into the lair of the Philistines. But what other options were there? A man had to hold to certain standards. At times it had not been easy but nevertheless he had stuck to his principles. It was what drove him in his efforts to rescue Turlough. And then he laughed.

'What a hypocrite you are, Halkias,' he said out loud. 'Samson wanted revenge for the wrongs the Philistines had done him. Don't fool yourself. You are a killer. Black and his pet dogs slew your brother and you will fill as many graves as it takes. They must pay, they must bleed.'

The township appeared ahead and Cyriac kept a steady pace towards the meeting with his enemies.

'There will be blood,' he muttered as he passed the town boundary.

There were four gunmen waiting on the porch of the hotel. They gave the rider hard looks through narrowed eyes; hands on gun butts.

Cyriac stepped down and took his time, pointedly adjusting his gun belt so it settled low on his hips. Then, ignoring the quartet of unfriendly gunnies, he strode up the steps and pushed open the door to the lobby.

Three more gunmen were sitting around, suddenly alert as Cyriac entered. Behind the desk was a nervous looking clerk. Cyriac strode over to him.

'My name is Cyriac Halkias. I've an appointment with Elwood Black.'

'Yes, sir,' the man said with a trembling voice. 'Mr Black is expecting you. Suite number seven. First floor.'

'Thank you.'

Turning from the desk, he was aware of the mounting tension in the lobby. Paying no attention to the gunnies intently watching him, he strode towards the stairs. There were two more on the landing. He tried to ignore them but they barred his progress. All bore the hallmarks of gunmen with tied down holsters and mean looking eyes.

'Halkias?' one of them said.

'I'm here to see Black.'

'You gotta hand over your weapons afore you go in.'

Cyriac stared implacably back, not saying anything. It made the gunmen nervous. Slowly he undid his gun belt with the holstered Remington and handed it over.

'The knife.'

Cyriac drew out the big Bowie, holding it a moment as if he wanted to stick it in something – preferably something living. The men before him tensed but in the end he handed it over.

'Move your hands out from your sides.'

They thought for a moment he was not going to comply but slowly he lifted his arms. They lifted the Mook from his shoulder holster and the Starr from where it was secured in the small of his back.

'You sure are loaded for bear, mister. Turn around.'

They made a thorough search before stepping aside and allowing him to proceed. He stopped at number seven, opened the door and entered.

Doctor McCullough and Arlene were seated opposite the door along with an older woman Cyriac took to be Mrs Richards. Their hands were roped together, resting on their laps. Two gunmen stood either side of them, their guns held casually – the threat obvious. Two more gunmen were standing either side of the door and turned to face Cyriac as he entered. Black was lounging on a chair with a smug look on his face.

'You shouldn't have come,' Doctor McCullough said.

Cyriac said nothing but walked to the window and looked outside, noting the balcony running the length of the hotel. At last he turned back to the room and leaned against the window frame.

'I was told you wanted to meet with me,' he said. 'What's it all about?'

'In order to make this a more amiable discourse, how about I ask you if you are armed?' Black said. 'Having witnessed you in action, I know how temperamental you can be.'

Cyriac held his arms wide. 'Your hound dogs made sure of that. What is this about?'

With a slight smirk, Black indicated a chair in the middle of the room. 'Sit.'

Cyriac pointed to the hostages. 'Are these people necessary to our talk?'

'I know from experience you are a very dangerous hombre, Halkias. These people have agreed to act as guarantors against any hostile action on your part. You cut up rough; your folk get roughed up, too. Maybe my boys might get carried away in the heat of the action and fire off a few shots. Anyone might get killed. You wouldn't want something like that on your conscience now, would you?'

Cyriac said nothing, staring steadily at the mine owner.

'Mr Halkias,' Black continued, 'ever since you came to Thomaston, you have caused me considerable inconvenience. Like I say, you are a very dangerous man. So instead of fighting you I have decided to give you an easy way out of this bind.'

'That's mighty big of you.'

'I am willing to forget all the trouble you have caused me and extend the hand of friendship,' Black continued.

144

'Let bygones be bygones, so to say.'

'So now you got me here helpless as a hogtied calf ready for branding, why don't you send these good people home.'

'All in good time. We got some talking to do first. As we know, you got a claim out at Gold Point, in joint ownership with a wanted murderer, Turlough Benedict. I need you to sign over your share of the mine to me. Once you do that we let these people go.'

Cyriac bent his head and stared at the floor for what seemed a long time. He could feel that familiar coldness rising up in the nape of his neck. The icy calmness spreading through his body. He made an effort to dampen it but it was growing and there was nothing he could do to prevent it. Only violence would exorcise it. Eventually he raised his head.

'I guess I got no other choice,' he said tightly. 'You have me over a barrel. You got anyone as can draw up the agreement?'

## 33

Black picked up a document from a table and handed the paper to Cyriac, who took it and scanned the writing.

'Looks like you hold all the aces. What happens to me after I sign?'

'You promise not to make any more trouble and you ride outta here and never come back, we lose interest in you.'

Cyriac nodded thoughtfully. 'You got a pen?'

Black picked up a pen, dipped it in an inkpot and handed it over. Holding the paper on his knee, Cyriac started to write, stopped and examined his efforts.

'Hell, I need something to lean on.'

He got up and moved over to the table, that coldness inside his head slowing everything around him. His muscles, shards of ice, were aching to explode and he had to prevent himself from bellowing out loud. Instead he swivelled on one foot and stabbed Black in the throat with the pen and at the same time, reaching out with his other hand and pulling the businessman into him.

The pen was rammed so hard it went in under Black's chin and up into his mouth, jamming his tongue into the back of his throat. Cyriac threw himself back, still holding the stricken man, reaching over and finding Black's gun in the shoulder holster. The gun came away easily and he sighted on the other gunnies and began firing. Black was gagging and gasping for breath, blood and snot blocking his damaged airway as he struggled futilely in Cyriac's fierce grip.

Cyriac's shots blasted out extraordinarily loudly in the confines of the room. The two gunmen guarding the hostages cried out as bullets hammered into them. Someone was rashly firing back – the bullets striking Black. The businessman arched his back and shuddered as he was hit. Cyriac, with a massive effort, pushed him on to his feet. Still holding Black, he rushed across the few feet and cannoned into the one gunman still standing – pushing Black into the man and knocking him off balance. By now Cyriac's gun was empty and he used it to lash out, catching his new opponent across the face with the barrel.

With Black thrashing about, hindering him, the gunman couldn't bring his gun to bear and Cyriac used his

146

empty weapon to smash it from his hand. He then dived to the floor, grappling for the fallen gun. One of the wounded gunmen was angling to get his weapon lined up on Cyriac.

He rolled over and fired at the same time. The slugs took the man in the eye and he jerked back, blood and brains spilling on to the carpet. Out of the corner of his eye, he saw another man bringing up his gun and got off a shot, putting a bullet in his gun hand. The injured man yelled and tried to swap over to his uninjured paw. It was a futile effort as one of Cyriac's shots hit him in the shoulder and the slug tossed him sideways. Another shot hit him in the head and he stopped moving.

Cyriac scrambled across the floor, picking up a chair and jamming it under the door handle. He was just in time as he heard men from outside shouting. Someone banged on the door.

'Mr Black, Mr Black, what's going on?'

'It's all right,' Cyriac called in what he hoped was an imitation of the mine owner's voice. 'Everything's under control.'

He found a knife on a gunman's unconscious body and began sawing at the captives' bonds.

'Climb out the window on the veranda,' he hissed as he worked. 'There'll be a stairway down to the street.'

The hammering on the door was getting louder, the yells from the corridor becoming more insistent.

'Mr Black!' called a voice.

Mrs Richards was staring in horror at the blood stained bodies strewn across the room.

'Go on – get,' Cyriac urged as he freed the doctor.

'Goddamn you, Cyriac, you sure are hell on wheels when it comes to killing.'

Before he could stop her, Arlene threw her arms around

147

him and squeezed him hard.

'Thank you, thank you,' she murmured in his ear, her soft breath caressing him at the same time. He pushed her towards the window now lying open with the doctor waiting beside it.

'Just get away from here,' Cyriac told them. 'Go somewhere safe.'

He turned and scanned the floor where the bodies of the men he had just shot were lying. The hammering on the door was becoming persistent.

'Mr Black, what the hell's going on?'

'It's all right, we're coming out,' he called back.

He had collected three guns from the floor and was rapidly reloading them. As a bonus he discovered a Colt .45 fully loaded.

One more glance out of the window and he could see no sign of Doctor McCullough and the two women. There was a noise from Black. The mining boss was gazing up at him, his hand clasped to his throat. He was trying to say something, the pen embedded in his throat preventing him from speaking and hindering his breathing. Cyriac bent over the injured man.

'I can't make out what you are saying,' he said. 'I gave you that pen so you could write to me when you get to hell. Let me know what it's like. Say hello to Old Nick for me. Tell him I'll be along sometime soon.'

Slowly the light faded from Black's eyes and he was left staring up accusingly at Cyriac.

'You sent out the men who slew my brother and now you have paid for that. However, it was your hound dog Carter who beat him so badly he died. When I catch up with him he'll be following you to hell.'

Cyriac stood and turned to face the door. He had a fully loaded Colt in each hand – his face set in a bleak mask.

'I guess there is some accounting still to be done in that respect,' he whispered into the empty room as the door shook under the hammering of the gunmen outside.

# 34

'We can't just sit here and let him go in there all alone to face those coyotes,' Aimee said to no one in particular.

'It's what he wanted,' Beth said. 'I feel as helpless as you but what can we do?'

'We could go in and lend him a hand,' Aimee persisted.

'That would be a dumb move,' Turlough said. 'We go in after him and spook Black into doing something really bad. You heard what Cyriac said. This thing is between him and Black.'

'You poor, pathetic piece of yeller dung,' Aimee sneered. She got to her feet and picked up her shotgun. 'I'm going into Thomaston. Maybe I can help Cyriac and maybe not but I sure as hell ain't going to cower here like no cowardly whipped dog and let him face them hell hounds all alone.'

Beth stood, too.

'We ought to go, I reckon,' she said. 'Poor Arlene and Mrs Roberts may need our help. What a snake that Black is, using females to blackmail Cyriac. There's every chance he'll murder all of them. Black's like a mad dog that's lashing out at anyone as comes near him.'

'We hurt him where it hurts most by wrecking his mining operation,' Aimee attested. 'He's a dog that needs putting down. The time for talking is over.'

Aimee stalked to the door. Beth threw on her coat and followed. Muttering under his breath, Turlough grabbed up his gun belt and went after them. They saddled up the horses and took the road into town, riding in grim silence. On the outskirts of Thomaston, Turlough drew rein.

'We don't know what we are riding into,' he said. 'All we know is that Cyriac was told to go to the hotel. Maybe we should leave the horses here and go in on foot.'

It was then they heard the gunfire.

'To hell with that,' Aimee yelled. 'We go straight in.'

And suiting action to words, she dug heels into her horse and set off at a run into the town.

'Hell, damn it, wait!' Turlough yelled but was forced to follow with Beth trailing behind.

Aimee hit the main street at a run and saw the gunmen on the hotel porch with their backs to her. Their attention was on something in the hotel. Then she saw the men all had shooters in their hands.

Not stopping to think, she dragged her shotgun from the thong on the saddle and as she rode past, she fired off both barrels into the crowded porch. Not waiting to see the effect of her actions, Aimee kept going and rounded a corner before anyone could react to her attack.

She left behind complete chaos as the buckshot splattered into the gunmen. Men fell, though none were fatally hurt. Some tried to get inside the hotel while others swung around, seeking their assailant and firing into the street.

Turlough, seeing the action, hauled on his reins and pulled up, blocking Beth from going any further and swinging around, urged both horses back the way they came. A few shots were fired after them but they turned into a side street where they dismounted.

'We'll go around the back of the hotel and try and find

150

out what's happening,' Turlough yelled.

Leaving the horses, they skirted the back alleys, heading towards the hotel, all the time listening apprehensively to noise of gunfire. Before they got to their objective, they ran into a group coming the other way.

'Doctor McCullough,' Turlough exclaimed. 'Where's Cyriac?'

'He's back there in the hotel,' the doctor panted. 'Lend me a gun and I'm going back there to help him. He's holed up there with a pack of wolves ready to tear him to pieces.'

Before Turlough could reply, he spied Aimee coming towards them, still mounted.

'What's happening?' she yelled and dropped down beside them.

'Doc says Cyriac is holed up in the hotel with a crowd of gunnies holding him at bay,' Turlough replied. 'We ought to help him.'

'I put a couple of barrels into the crowd at the front of the hotel.' Aimee was pushing more shells into her weapon. 'That ought to pare them down a mite.'

'Damn it to hell, I need a gun,' the doctor grumbled. 'Ain't any of you got a spare?'

'Here.' Beth pulled a pistol from beneath her coat. 'This will be more useful to you than me.'

The doctor eagerly took the weapon, checked the loads and looked up at his companions, his eyes bright and eager.

'Let's give those fellas hell.'

Cyriac emptied his borrowed Colt into the closed door – the bullets punching through the flimsy wood panels. He heard screams and curses from outside and yells of anger. There was the thud of a body falling to the floor. Then the sound of running boots as the gunnies fled out of danger.

Tossing the empty weapon to the floor, Cyriac grabbed another Colt and strode over to the wrecked door. Keeping to one side out of the line of fire in case any of the gunmen thought of firing back, Cyriac kicked away the chair blocking it. Still keeping well to one side, he pulled open the ruined door. Curling his hand around the door frame and without looking, he fired off a few shots. There was no response so he squatted down and risked a peep into the corridor. Other than the dead gunman lying in a pool of blood, the corridor was clear.

Keeping a cautious look out both ways, Cyriac stepped through the doorway and fished a Webley five shot from the hand of the dead gunman and stuffed it in his belt. Warily he walked along the corridor with a gun clenched in each fist, expecting any moment gunmen to appear and start firing back at him. Arriving on the deserted landing, he paused. Piled in a heap were the weapons that had been taken from him when he arrived at the hotel.

He shucked the borrowed guns and checking to make sure they had not been tampered with, he armed himself with his own weapons, tucking the Bowie into its sheath.

'Your boss is dead,' he yelled out. 'If you want to keep fighting for a dead man, that's your choice. I'm coming down and any man I find with a gun in his hand I will kill. I've already killed all your buddies in room seven.'

Slowly he began to descend the stairs, expecting any moment an outbreak of gunfire but all remained quiet. With a quick leap he was at the bottom of the stairs, guns sweeping the lobby, trigger fingers ready. Where he had expected a horde of gunnies there was no sign of anyone. As far as he could see the lobby was empty. There was a faint noise behind him and he swung around, firing off two rounds but there was nothing there.

'Come out, whoever you are,' he called.

From behind the reception desk, a hand came up and slowly moved back and forth.

'Don't shoot. I'm only the messenger,' a quavering voice answered.

The other empty hand appeared followed by a head and then, visibly shaking, the hotel clerk stood upright.

'I have a message from Clive Carter. I've to tell you to look out in the street.'

Cyriac walked to the window and risked a peek outside. Aimee was sitting in the dirt while the doctor worked on a bloody wound in her leg with Beth assisting. Turlough's shirt was blood-soaked and Mrs Roberts and Arlene were supporting him, one on each side. Arranged across the street were armed men with guns trained on the little group.

'I see them,' he said, the cold rage growing in his head and spreading.

'If you don't come out and surrender, he says his men will kill your people.'

# 35

Cyriac stood at the window, his eyes scanning the buildings opposite, craning his neck to take in as much as was visible from his vantage point. He could see men sheltering in doorways and counted up to six.

'Which one is Carter? Describe him to me.'

'He is a big fella, with dark eyes and a mop of red hair.'

'How's he dressed?'

'He wears a black low crowned hat with a silver band. In fact, come to think of it, he dresses all in black.'

Cryiac narrowed his eyes, thinking deeply, trying to figure a way out of his predicament. Before he could come to any conclusion he heard someone shouting his name. He walked to the door and pushed it open, making sure to keep under cover.

'Yes, this is Halkias.'

'What do you want?' the voice called.

'I've come here to kill Clive Carter,' Cyriac answered. 'He murdered my brother.'

'I'm Carter,' the voice called back. 'How do you know it was me as killed your brother?'

'You were seen. Let those folk go. They ain't part of this vendetta. This is just between you and me.'

'Is that so? Well, they bought into it just the same. They were on the way to rescue you when they ran into me. Tough! We finish this here and now. Either you come out and surrender or we kill your people.'

Cyriac stared at the sorry group in the street, wounded and helpless.

His people, Carter had said. But he had no people. He only had Milo and Milo was dead. Yet the phrase stuck in his mind – his people!

Turlough hounded because he was heir to a valuable gold claim.

Beth and Aimee thrown by mischance into the group, not flinching when it came to helping him keep Turlough alive.

Doctor McCullough, a man doing his best to practice his medicine in a crooked town and keep his daughter safe.

And then there was Arlene. Before she left the hotel she had hugged him.

His people!

'I have no people,' he whispered.

But the more he looked out at that pitiful group in the street, the less he was able to believe he was not responsible for their fate.

A shot rang out and Cyriac saw the dirt kicked up in the road in front of the little band.

'Time's running out, Halkias,' Carter called.

'They tell me you are a fast man with a gun, Carter,' Cyriac called back.

'The best. I'm still alive while I got a tally of fifteen men who thought they were better than me.'

'That's impressive. Fifteen! How's about you and I shoot it out? Just you and me – man to man.'

'No chance, Halkias. I got you over a barrel. You got nowhere to go. The only thing certain is that you have a chance to save your folk if you give yourself up.'

'I thought as much. Gunnies like you are lily-livered scum hiding behind a gang. Back-shooters that only come out from under their rotten log when the odds are in their favour. I doubt you killed fifteen men face to face. More than likely sneaked up and shot at them from a dark alley while your gang put in a few shots to make it safe for you to crawl outta your hole.'

'That's a lie. I ain't no back-shooter.'

'Is that so? Black told me if I got out of the hotel alive I needed to watch my back because Clive Carter would come one night and bushwhack me.'

'Elwood never said no such thing.' There was an edge of anger in Carter's voice.

'He can't say one way or another cos I killed him like I kill anyone as comes up against me. I killed Ginsburg and Linenan and a host of your buddies. I guess that's why you're scared to face me.'

155

'I ain't afraid of no man.' The anger was rising.

'Back-shooters are the lowest form of life crawling on this earth. They're like maggots – feeding on cadavers. I guess they have a special smell, too. Let me guess, you probably wear black so as you can sneak about at night and do your killing. You're scared now, ain't you, Clive? Your men watching and listening and they know the truth. You're afraid to come out in the daylight to do your killing. Huh, I bet those fifteen you killed were mostly women and children. Did you have to sneak up on them while they weren't watching?'

'I ain't no woman killer, you son of a bitch. Come out and face me and I'll show you who's afraid.'

'Sure thing, Carter the Coward. You got all your men ranged around so they can shoot me up a mite to make it easier for you.'

'I do my own killing, you son of a bitch.'

'Stand your men down and come out and face me.'

There was no reply and Cyriac waited.

'You heard him, men,' Carter called eventually. 'You go on down the saloon. I'll follow on as soon as I kill this big-mouth son of a bitch.'

Cyriac watched the men step out from cover.

'You sure about this, Clive?'

'Do as I tell you. I'll make short work of this blowhard.'

They went, holstering guns as they walked down the street in the direction of The Golden Nugget. As the last of them moved away, Cyriac stepped out on to the boardwalk. He had located the direction from which Carter's voice had originated and he was watchful for any sign of treachery from the gunman.

'Cyriac,' Arlene called. 'Don't do this.'

'He's a killer,' the doctor added.

Cyriac held up his hand, palm towards them, in a

156

gesture of reassurance.

'Go on home now. Attend to your hurts. This has got to end now.'

A dark clad figure stepped into sight further down the street. Clive Carter, renowned gunfighter with fifteen notches on his gun, came out into the street to add another name to the list of men he had killed.

Cyriac holstered his guns. The group in the road had not done as he had told them. They were waiting to see the outcome of the gunfight. Cyriac started walking.

A silence descended on that street so quiet Cyriac's footsteps sounded loud like the slow beat of a drum as he stalked towards the killer. Carter stood in the road, his hands poised over his guns. He wore crossed gun belts with tied down holsters sporting twin Colt Peacemakers with inlaid pearl handles. He was almost as tall as Cyriac but not as bulky, having a sinewy build.

'Time to die, greaseball,' Carter called.

Cyriac said nothing, walking grimly on, narrowing the gap between himself and the killer.

'That's far enough,' the gunman warned. 'I don't want your blood soiling my shirt.'

Still Cyriac remained silent, steadily pacing along the street, the distance between the men narrowing. Cyriac's hands stayed by his sides, not swinging as he walked bent slightly forward as if eager to close with Carter.

'I said that's far enough!' There was a hint of edginess in Carter's voice.

Cyriac was seemingly indifferent as he stalked forward, neither hurrying nor dallying, steadily getting closer and closer to the gunman. They were only yards apart and still Cyriac came on. It was too much for Carter. His hands dipped and he snatched his guns from their holsters.

Cyriac moved too, his arm coming up with bewildering speed, the light glinting on steel as the big Bowie left his hand in an underarm throw, spinning through the air and driving into Carter's throat, throwing him back. Blood welling up, spurting in a crimson streak down his front.

One gun fired, well wide of its target, but then Cyriac was on the gunman, punching Carter in the chest with a powerful blow that lifted him from his feet and dumped him on his back. Carter lay staring up at his attacker, the handle of the Bowie jutting from his throat. He was trying to bring his guns into play. Cyriac straddled the wounded man, a boot on each hand, Carter's guns useless as the weight of the huge man crushed his fingers into the dirt.

Cyriac reached down and pulled the knife free, blood dripping from the blade. Carter opened his mouth as if to say something but all that emerged was a bubble of blood. His eyes were wide, staring at the man who had just defeated him.

Clive Carter, feared gunman, had been beaten to the draw by a knife but it was no ordinary knife. The Bowie was a knife designed for killing, the steel blade nine inches long and honed to razor sharpness.

Cyriac crouched bent over the dying man.

'You won't be lonely in hell, Carter. Elwood Black and Sheriff Ginsburg are waiting for you to join them. Give them my regards.'

The light faded from the dying man's eyes and all movement stopped. Cyriac wiped the blade of his knife on the gunman's shirt and stepped back, looking up the street in the direction of the saloon. A group of Carter's gunnies stood on the boardwalk, staring down at him.

Casually Cyriac bent and plucked Carter's twin guns from his ruined hands and stood holding them. Moments passed and then without a word, the gunmen turned and one by one stepped back inside the saloon. When the swing doors ceased moving, Cyriac tossed the guns on to the dead man's chest, turned and walked back towards the group by the hotel.

'Let's get you inside,' he said, bending down and taking Aimee under the arm. 'How's the leg?'

Aimee could not reply, for she was gritting her teeth against the pain. Doctor McCullough took her other arm and together they helped her into the hotel.

Behind came Turlough assisted by Beth. There was a slight disturbance from behind and Cyriac looked over his shoulder to see the storekeeper holding a weeping Mrs Roberts in a tight embrace. The man looked towards Cyriac and nodded.

Arlene was kept busy, helping her father attend to the wounded. She appropriated bed sheets from the hotel, tearing them into strips as makeshift bandages and pestering the clerk for hot water. During a break, she looked around for Cyriac and not seeing him, asked her father where he was.

'Don't know,' he said. 'I've been too busy to notice anything other than patching up these two.'

'I saw him go out the front,' Turlough said.

A bullet had gone through the right side of his chest, not doing any serious damage. Arlene had a sudden premonition and quickly went outside. There was no sign of Cyriac.

Roberts the storekeeper was tending to his wife on the porch. A bottle of brandy was on the floor and both had filled glasses. Mrs Roberts was red eyed from weeping and her husband had a protective arm around her.

'Have you seen Cyriac?' she asked.

Roberts pointed vaguely down the street. 'I saw him go in that direction a while back.'

Arlene picked up her skirts and started running but stopped when she saw the horseman.

'Cyriac!' she yelled. 'Cyriac!'

The horse stopped and he wheeled about and watched as she closed the distance between them.

'Where are you going?' she panted, out of breath.

He stared down at her and she knew then he was leaving.

'Miss Arlene, there is no place for me here. I have done what I came here to do and now I must move on.'

'Don't go,' she pleaded. 'I want you to stay.'

He bowed his head, looking down at his scarred hands folded on the pommel of saddle. So ugly and misshapen. He held them up.

'Miss Arlene, take a good look at these hands. They are killer's hands. They have done terrible deeds over the years. You are a lovely, refined young woman. You deserve someone better than me. I am no fit companion for respectable folk like you and your pa.'

'I don't care.' There were tears in her eyes as she gazed ardently up at him. 'A man can change.'

'Find yourself a good man, Miss Arlene – someone more deserving of you.'

He picked up the reins and tugged the horse's head about and nudged it forward, away from Arlene.

'Cyriac,' she called.

But he kept riding stiff-backed. She stood in the road, a lonely figure watching him ride out of her life.